STILL LIFE

NINE STORIES

BY

NICHOLAS KAUFMANN

Something moved beneath the skin of her leg, twisting around the muscle like a vine. Her breath caught in her throat.

Set it free. Cut it out of you and take control.

She pressed the razor to her soft, pale thigh. She held her breath, afraid, then slashed it sideways as hard as she could. A line of blood followed the razor's trail, dribbling down her leg and into the water, where it spread out in waving tendrils like red smoke. The sharp pain only lasted a moment before dulling, but during that moment her heart drummed, her skin tingled, and she felt more alive, more herself, than she had in years. Pain broke the walls of the cocoon she'd spun around herself, and the sensation waiting on the other side belonged to her, no one else.

In pain you are perfection. Now set it free.

She gasped as the skin around the cut bulged suddenly. What was happening? Had she cut too deep, slashed an important artery? It hurt worse than the razor slice. The pain seemed to whisper her name.

The edges of the slit puckered open like lips. Something long and black dropped out, landing in the water with a heavy splash. Christine kicked against the bathmat, trying to get out of the tub without touching the oily black eel that now swam around her ankles. She grabbed the edge of the tub, ready to pull herself over onto the tiled bathroom floor, but the eel changed course, torpedoing up along her torso. It surfaced, its slick, black, eyeless head splitting apart into spiky jaws.

PUBLICATION HISTORY

For Alexa, always.

Special thanks to all the members of Who Wants Cake, past and present. Special thanks also to the editors who first took a risk on the stories in this collection: Richard Chizmar, Jesus Gonzalez, Michael Laimo, Dave Lindschmidt, Robert Morrish, Garrett Peck, Judi Rohrig, and Heather Shaw. A big thank you to James A. Moore for the flattery, and to Bob Booth, Matt Bechtel, and everyone else who's involved with Necon E-Books. And last, but not at all least, my heartfelt thanks to all of you, my readers. Your support through the years has meant more to me than I can possibly say.

CONTENTS

INTRODUCTION: DARK NOTES

BY JAMES A. MOORE

You want to know what I like about different writers? They aren't the same. No, it's not a joke; I'm deadly serious. There is nothing more desperately frustrating to me than reading seven different authors who sound alike. I mean they have the same tempo, that they have the same notes and can easily be confused for one another, or, worse, confused for the same source material that they are trying so desperately to imitate.

I was interviewed recently and the interviewer said he could tell my particular voice by the rhythm of the words. I guess, honestly, you have to be an avid reader or just possibly a writer to really understand that, but it's true. There's a rhythm and at the end of it all the words are like dancing. And my God, what a miserable world if every dance were the same.

The difference is in the rhythm, the tempo, and the beat of the story.

Nicholas Kaufmann is a damned fine composer. And that interviewer was right. You can read a story by Kaufmann and you can hear the rhythm he's writing to. It's not the same as mine, or really very much like anyone else's that I've run across. That, to me, is a sign of excellence. Oh, don't get me wrong. I've run across a lot of good stories that were written down and qualified as solid tales. They worked well enough. Some of them might even have qualified as literature (and I say that while still contending that literature is a happy coincidence and seldom something that can be achieved with any deliberation, but that's a debate for another time). But the thing about those stories is, you can't dance to them. I don't mean with your foot, of course, but with your imagination. They do not fire the mind's eye, and they don't satisfy me the way a really good tale by a truly skilled composer does.

Kaufmann, on the other hand, is a writer you can dance to. Damn, but he's got a way with words and imagery. Try this little note on for size: "She swallowed her anger. It tasted bitter, thorny, and she felt it slither down the muscles under her skin." That's just sweet. That's a small taste of imagery that lingers, and that you can hear when you're reading. I read that sentence the first time and I had to stop reading, because I needed to not only feel that rhythm Kaufmann was setting up, but I also felt a nearly desperate need to understand how he got the lyrics to match so damned perfectly with the beat of his words.

These stories span eleven years, more than a decade, and they have certain things in common. Universally, they are excellent tales. They should be. Kaufmann is smart enough to know what stories to put in a collection. If he's anything like me there are a few tales he has locked away in a dark place that no one, and I mean no one, ever gets to see. We all have a few of those pieces, I suspect. We'd like to get rid of them, but, really, they are our children, no matter how much they caterwaul and wail and fall away from the songs we're doing our best to write.

There are no cacophonous pieces here. These are masterpieces. Each and every one of them is a worthy companion to their counterparts. I'll take my analogy one step further for you: these separate pieces work together like the very best musical albums: they compliment each other and make a whole that is larger and more complete than the sum of its parts.

There are nine stories here. Nine pieces of music, each of them unique, each of them, frankly, powerful. I will not go on about each tale. I will not, much as I want to, explain why I was so deeply moved by "The Jew of Prague," or why "The Beat of Her Wings" was so damned delicious. I won't carefully examine the notes that complete "Under the Skin," which I quoted from above, because that's not what I'm here for. I'm here to introduce the work, not break it down for you. Words, like music, are often a personal thing. I can share a song with a crowd of people, but each of them will take something different from that song. Music is subjective, after all.

But they have something in common, these tales. They are told with a masterful skill. They are composed with a rhythm that is unique to Nicholas Kaufmann. Listen carefully as you read, and you'll hear that rhythm, catch the tempo written in notes of human suffering and a careful examination of the darkness that hides inside the tales Kaufmann has written.

To me that rhythm is almost perfectly in sync with a heartbeat.

Damn, I envy Kaufmann that. Masterful. Absolutely masterful.

James A. Moore
August 2012

UNDER THE SKIN

Like many authors, I'm ridiculously critical of everything I write. I look back on some of my work, especially my older work, with harsh judgment. However, that's not the case with "Under the Skin." I happen to think this story is one of the best I've written. It was originally published in a magazine that featured urban-set horror stories interspersed with photos of scantily clad goth models (don't you just love this genre?). Alas, the magazine only lasted a handful of issues. It didn't have a very big readership, and that meant "Under the Skin" wasn't read by as many people as I would have liked. Now, finally, it's getting a second chance. Notably, it's one of the few stories I've written that draws upon my Jewish background. Luckily, none of my family's Passover seders were anything like this one.

Christine looks across the table at Karin, but her twin sister is too busy perusing the prayer book Dad handed out when they sat down for dinner. (Haggadah, he called it, having rediscovered his Jewish roots after the separation.) She stares at the top of Karin's head until her sister glances up at her. Karin brushes back the long blonde hair that falls in her face, the same hair Christine used to have before the cut and dye job, and says, "Stop staring at me, Vampirella!"

Instinctively, Christine looks to her father at the head of the table to say something, but he doesn't tell Karin to behave herself; he just pours wine like nothing happened. At the foot of the table, as far from Dad as the rectangular table allows, her mother doesn't say anything, either, only sighs and crosses her legs, clearly annoyed at herself for accepting Dad's invitation.

That neither of them scold Karin is no surprise to Christine. Her sister can break the rules without getting caught because she has Mom and Dad wrapped around her finger. Karin has always been the favorite twin. Mom even gave birth to her first, as if to prove her devotion.

Her mother glares at Christine as if to say, "I can't believe you put that thing through your eyebrow." Self-conscious, Christine touches the ring above her left eye and looks away.

Dad's new apartment has a better smell than the one she shares with Karin and Mom, all musky leather furniture and new plastic electronics. Watching him tip the dark green wine bottle over his glass, Christine feels a sudden pang of loss. He doesn't call or email much, and even now, with the two of them sitting at the same table, he's not paying attention to her. When they first walked in, he asked Karin all about her plans for the summer between Junior and Senior years of high school, about her friends and social life, but all Christine got was, "What happened to your hair?"

Dad puts the bottle down. "This is the best part of the Passover seder," he explains, picking up the Haggadah next to his plate. "Well, except for actually eating dinner, which I promise will be soon." He grins. Mom sighs again and looks longingly at the apartment door. "Every time one of the plagues of Egypt is mentioned, what you do is dip your finger in the wine and put a drop on your plate. The spilling of the wine reminds us that our cup of joy is not complete because people died for our freedom from slavery." He flips open the Haggadah and reads from it, "From the house of bondage we went forth to freedom. These are the ten plagues that The Holy One, blessed be He, brought upon Pharaoh and his people in Egypt." He dips his pinky in the wine glass, then touches the finger to his plate, leaving a small, purple bead.

"Dam," he says, pronouncing the Hebrew perfectly. "Blood."

Christine remembers blood:

Standing naked in front of the bathroom mirror, all Christine saw, all she ever saw, was Karin. They were physically identical in every way. The same bony hips, the same woefully underdeveloped chest that she secretly hoped would fill out before her sister's, the same straight blonde hair hanging limply down to her too-narrow shoulders.

"Grounded," she whispered to her reflection. All because she'd flunked some stupid assignment for her Bible As Literature class. She'd written a paper about how Moses was schizo because he heard voices no one else did. She got it back with a big red F and the words "You're not taking Exodus very seriously" scrawled across the top.

"You're not leaving this house until your grades improve," Mom had said. "I won't have my daughter going to community college. Karin's getting straight As, why can't you?"

"Because I'm not Karin," she said now, despite the face she saw in the bathroom mirror. "I'm Christine, the fucked up twin. The medical miracle. The one no one expected to survive." Mom loved telling the story about how the doctors thought she would be smothered sharing the womb with her stronger, healthier, umbilical-hogging sister—it was her way of reminding Christine that from the very start she'd always been the weaker daughter. But she had survived, and when she was born it was like it was too late, like her parents had already decided not to get too attached to her. Her sister was no comfort. Instead of the bond between identical twins she'd heard so much about, their relationship had been confrontational and competitive since day one, like they were still fighting for legroom in utero. She didn't want to be anything like her. She just wanted to be free of her. Sometimes she wished the doctors had been right.

And now she was grounded and couldn't go out with Alan Healy, the only boy in school who seemed to like her, even though she wrote angry poetry and smoked cloves in the girls' bathroom. She'd seen him peeking at her from around corners and behind books, and now that he'd finally worked up the nerve to ask her out, she couldn't go. Meanwhile, Karin, who'd never cracked a textbook in her life and probably blew teachers in alleys to get her straight As, got to go out and enjoy herself. It wasn't fair.

Christine clenched her fists. She swallowed her anger. It tasted bitter, thorny, and she felt it slither down the muscles under her skin.

She stepped into the tub and sat in the warm water. She lathered soap up and down her legs and grabbed the pink plastic razor next to the soap dish. She pulled it along her left leg from ankle to thigh, carving a trail through the thick white lather.

Mom's voice floated in from the living room. Christine could tell from the way she yelled that she was on the phone with Dad. "I do everything I can to keep this family going! No, it's not Karin, it's your other daughter, as usual."

A sting, a flash of red where the razor cut her, and Christine sucked air in through her teeth. She looked at the tiny crimson spot on her leg. She touched the blood with one finger.

Hello, Christine. The voice, deep and smooth, seemed to echo off the white tile walls and the inside of her skull.

"Who's there?" She leaned out of the tub, dripping sudsy water onto the floor. The bathroom was empty. She scrunched her eyes closed as hard as she could. "Wake up," she whispered to herself.

You're not like your sister, Christine. Not anymore. Open your eyes and let me show you how.

She opened her eyes slowly.

See the cut on your leg? That's what sets you apart.

The red spot against her skin looked beautiful, like a frosted rose on a birthday cake she'd never have to share.

But ask yourself, Christine, is it enough? The cut was an accident. She's bound to have shaving cuts, too.

"No, I'm not listening," Christine said, covering her face. The hard handle of the razor pressed against her cheek.

She could have the very same cut you do. Then how would you be different?

"Stop it." She put her hands over her ears. "There's no one here. You're not real."

You can't rely on random accidents to set you apart from her, Christine. You need to take control.

She lowered her hands and looked at the silver glint of metal in the razor's head.

Do it, Christine. Identical is only skin deep. It's what's under the skin that matters.

Something moved beneath the skin of her leg, twisting around the muscle like a vine. Her breath caught in her throat.

Set it free. Cut it out of you and take control.

She pressed the razor to her soft, pale thigh. She held her breath, afraid, then slashed it sideways as hard as she could. A line of blood followed the razor's trail, dribbling down her leg and into the water, where it spread out in waving tendrils like red smoke. The sharp pain only lasted a moment before dulling, but during that moment her heart drummed, her skin tingled, and she felt more alive, more herself, than she had in years. Pain broke the walls of the cocoon she'd spun around herself, and the sensation waiting on the other side belonged to her, no one else.

In pain you are perfection. Now set it free.

She gasped as the skin around the cut bulged suddenly. What was happening? Had she cut too deep, slashed an important artery? It hurt worse than the razor slice. The pain seemed to whisper her name.

The edges of the slit puckered open like lips. Something long and black dropped out, landing in the water with a heavy splash. Christine kicked against the bathmat, trying to get out of the tub without touching the oily black eel that now swam around her ankles. She grabbed the edge of the tub, ready to pull herself over onto the tiled bathroom floor, but the eel changed course, torpedoing up along her torso. It surfaced, its slick, black, eyeless head splitting apart into spiky jaws.

"Go away!" she screamed, splashing and kicking the walls of the tub. "Go away!"

The eel closed its mouth. It turned around and glided down toward the drain, bumping its head against the rubber plug that blocked its path. Christine rose to her knees. She pulled the chain, yanking the plug out of the drain, and the eel slid quickly down the dark hole.

Such a waste. You need to learn to take control, Christine.

She looked at the cut on her thigh. It had closed into a thin red line again.

Christine mimics her father, sinking her pinky into the warm wine and then touching it to her plate. The purple bead that rolls off her fingertip looks like the blood it's named after.

"Tzfardea, frogs," Dad continues, dipping again. "Kinim, lice."

Her finger is too wet now. Some of the wine drips onto her palm before she can tap it on the plate. She sticks her pinky in her mouth to clean it off.

"Whoa," Dad says. "You're not supposed to do that, Christine. Our cup of joy is not complete because people died, remember? It's considered insensitive to lick your finger because then it's like you're taking pleasure in it."

"Sorry," she says. Her cheeks burn.

"Passover is all about people dying so others can be set free," he says.

Christine wants to say, "The Book of Exodus," and wow everyone with what she learned in Bible As Lit, but Karin interrupts, "Idiot."

"Let's just get on with it," Mom says.

"Is there a problem, Elaine?" Dad asks. Christine flinches. There's an edge in his voice she's not used to anymore now that he's not living at home with them.

"No, Matt, there's no problem," Mom says, her voice extra saccharine. "Why don't you tell us more about your cup of joy?"

While her parents cut into each other, Karin leans forward, her collar coming away to reveal a dark hickey on her neck. She whispers across the table to Christine, "Alan cried like a baby afterward. I did you a favor, sparing you that pathetic display. He wasn't even very good."

"Fuck you," Christine snarls, a little too loud.

"Christine, that's enough," Dad says angrily. "Behave yourself at the table."

Karin smirks and flips her the finger when Mom and Dad aren't looking. Not that it would matter if they saw her. She gets away with everything.

"The sooner we finish this, the sooner we can eat," Dad says, picking up the Haggadah again.

"Hallelujah," Mom says.

Dad glares at her, then sticks his pinky in the wine glass. "Arov," he says, "beasts."

"When did you learn Hebrew anyway?" Mom asks, drinking freely from her wine glass. "You were never very good at learning new things."

"Dever," he continues. "Pestilence." The word slices through the air like a straightedge.

Frightened by the incident in the bathtub, Christine looked for new ways to distinguish herself from her twin sister. She raided her wardrobe and held a lonely midnight funeral behind the apartment building for her beaded V-neck tanks, fitted bellbottoms, and pink and blue topsiders. She replaced them with t-shirts with the sleeves cut off, camouflage pants, steel-toed black boots, and topped it all off with a frayed denim jacket. But it wasn't enough. Now she just looked like Karin in a Halloween costume. Something more drastic was necessary.

She surprised Alan with her new haircut shortly before the big Spring Fling dance. She'd chopped most of it off, shaved half of her head down to a fine fuzz, and dyed it all a deep black. "It feels more like me," she told him. Her heart sank when she saw his face. "You don't like it?" He hemmed and hawed and kicked at the ground with his sneakers. He couldn't break up with her fast enough.

Alan asked Karin to the dance instead, and her sister agreed to go.

"You know he only asked you to get back at me," she said, leaning against the doorframe of Karin's bedroom. "Because you look the way I used to."

She eyed the clock by the bed. Only half an hour until Alan came to pick Karin up for the dance. And what would Christine do then? Hide in her room until her sister and ex-boyfriend were gone? Sit in the bathtub and—

No, she thought. No more cutting. But in her head she saw the blade glinting prettily and wondered if it would feel as good now as it did the first time.

"I don't care," Karin replied, applying mascara at her makeup table. "I always thought Alan was a hottie. Is there anything I should know, like is he a bad kisser?"

"You're going to kiss my ex-boyfriend?"

Karin shrugged. "You had your chance with him, but you fucked it up with your stupid dyke haircut. Accept it and move on. Besides, it's almost the end of the year, and there's no way I'm going into Senior Year a virgin."

Christine furrowed her brow. "What are you talking about?"

Her sister rolled her eyes, opened a drawer in the table, and pulled out a condom in bright yellow wrapping. She held it up so Christine could see, then dropped it into her sequined purse. "Duh," Karin said.

Mom appeared in the doorway behind Christine. "Don't stay out too late tonight, Karin. We have your father's Jewish thing tomorrow."

"Don't worry," Karin said. She locked eyes with Christine. "I'm sure I'll be in bed early."

Christine clenched her fists. Something moved under her skin.

No way was she going to wait around for Alan to pick Karin up. She went downtown to get lost in the crowd instead, weaving around all the hand-holding couples and looking away whenever a white stretch limo drove by. The sound of muffled laughter behind the tinted windows disturbed her, as if each limo held Alan and Karin, as if they were circling the block, driving past her again and again to rub it in her face. First they were kissing in the back seat, and then, when they drove by again, Alan was whispering in Karin's ear, "It was always you I liked, not Christine. She's a freak. I just did what I had to do to get closer to you." And then, the next time, his hand was inside the top of her dress, and the time after that he was lying on top of her, doing things they'd never done while the driver tried not to watch in the rearview mirror.

"Like I care," Christine muttered. She walked the razor's edge of the sidewalk, hugging the buildings and keeping a buffer of people between her and the passing limos. She stopped in front of a storefront. "Wildside Tattoo & Piercing" was stenciled on the window. The glass shelves displayed all kinds of bulky silver jewelry: earrings, navel rings, lip rings, eyebrow rings. The store was practically empty, just a couple of college students looking through the tattoo design books and giggling nervously. Behind the counter, a big, bald man with a long beard and tattoo-covered arms looked bored. He met her gaze and raised one eyebrow.

Christine pulled open the heavy glass door and stepped inside. It smelled like cigarette smoke and ammonia. "Slow night?" she asked. Her own voice sounded too high to her, too young, and she made a show of clearing her throat.

"There's some kind of school dance or something," he said with a shrug. She liked his voice, it was thick and smooth like honey. He eyed the college kids shuffling closer to the door. "They're not gonna get anything tonight. I knew it the moment they walked in. Gawkers."

"Fuck 'em," she said. "Total poseurs."

He looked at her disdainfully. "And what are you?"

"The real deal," she said.

He looked her up and down. "If you say so." He introduced himself as Satyr. Christine nodded like it was no big deal, but secretly she thought it was the coolest thing she'd ever heard.

Five minutes later she was in the chair in back, ready to get her eyebrow pierced. Satyr switched on his iPod and stuffed the earbuds in his ears. Bobbing his head to music she couldn't hear, he washed his hands in the rust-stained sink and dried them on his leather vest. He wiped down the area above her left eye with alcohol. He pulled the skin away from her skull, held it there with a small clamp, then took a needle and a small metal hoop out of the drawer.

"Hold still, real deal, this is gonna hurt," he said.

"Pain and I go way back," Christine said, though she doubted he could hear anything over the music. She wished he would take out the earbuds and pay attention to her. He had the deepest brown eyes she'd ever seen. Just as she was wondering what it would feel like to run her fingers through his beard, he pushed the needle through the skin of her eyebrow.

Her fingernails dug into the upholstery of the armrests. She felt a drop of blood roll down the side of her face. He put the ring through the hole he'd made, then removed the clamp. He leaned forward to dab the blood from her face. Close up, his mouth looked soft. She wondered what it would be like to kiss him, but then he swiveled away on his chair to wash his tools in the sink. Christine released the armrests.

Satyr turned off his iPod and left it on the lip of the sink. He picked up a small, frameless mirror, then turned back to her. "What do you think?" he asked, though it didn't sound like he cared what her answer would be.

"Perfect. How much do I owe you?"

"Forty," he said, putting the mirror back under the sink.

She took a deep breath, steeling herself, and put a hand on his thigh. "That's a little steep. Maybe we can work something out?" She'd seen it in a movie once, though now she remembered the actress had said, "Maybe we can come to an arrangement," and her voice had been lower, too; smokier, more seductive. Christine wished she could start over and do it again the right way.

Satyr made a noise like steam escaping from a radiator. He picked her hand up and placed it back on her lap. "I think not. I have enough poseur girls who want to fuck me to piss off their mommies or boyfriends or whoever, I don't need another one. So why don't you break out the credit card you stole from daddy's wallet and we'll take it from there, okay?"

For a moment, she couldn't react. Then she turned away from him, angry that he might see her chin quivering. She asked if there was a bathroom, and he waved vaguely in the direction of the graffiti-covered doors in the back wall. She locked herself in the women's room, sat on the chipped toilet seat, and rummaged through her bag for tissues. She couldn't believe she was crying. What was she, a baby? No wonder Satyr rejected her. He probably thought she was just a little girl, utterly sexless.

Her fingers touched something hard tucked into the corner of her bag—a small pocketknife she'd gotten at the Army Navy store for a dollar. She took it out and flipped open the small, sharp blade.

Hello, Christine.

She dropped the knife. It clattered on the water-stained floor between her feet.

You remember what to do, don't you? Pick up the knife.

"Leave me alone," she whimpered. But her skin itched for the cut.

It's only natural, Christine. The whole world is cut up. Your parents. You and Alan. Everything is cut up and rearranged out of order.

It was true. Nothing was the way it was supposed to be.

Pick up the knife and take control.

She bent down and retrieved the pocketknife from the floor. She unbuttoned her camouflage pants, pushed them down past her knees.

Do it, Christine.

She held the blade to the skin of her right thigh. Shapes writhed eagerly beneath it.

Set it free.

"Oh God," she screamed, dragging the blade across her leg. It stung hot and cold at the same time.

Someone banged on the door. "Christ, kid, what are you doing in there?" Satyr's voice.

"Oh God," she cried again, the pain bringing relief. Ecstasy.

In pain you are perfection, Christine. Irresistible. All you have to do it take control.

She reached from where she sat and opened the bathroom door. Satyr rolled his eyes when he saw her sitting there with her pants down. Then he saw the blood, and the pocketknife in her hand. He stepped into the room.

"Oh Jesus, what did you...?"

She kicked the door closed behind him. The cut on her thigh bulged, puckered open. An oily black eel pushed its way out and slithered across her lap, landing on the bathroom floor with a heavy splat. It reared up like a cobra, its head splitting open into a terrible, spiky mouth. Then it sprang, disappearing under Satyr's vest.

He cried out, convulsed, then quieted.

He straightened up and looked at her expectantly.

The muscles of his face were slack. His eyes had clouded over a milky white. A black ichor oozed out from between his lips like paste.

Now, Christine.

She stood slowly. Satyr didn't move. Was he dead? What had the eel done to him? She touched his cheek. His skin felt cold, and he didn't react. She reached up and ran her hand along the hairs of his beard. So smooth, just like she knew it would be. This was the kind of man for her, not that wuss Alan Healy. Wusses were for Karin. This was a real man, and real men were for Christine.

Take control.

She felt tendrils of energy emanating from inside her, connecting her to Satyr, or maybe to the eel that had burrowed inside him. It was like holding a marionette in her hands. Pull a string and the puppet raises its arm. If she wanted to, she wondered, could she make him…?

He lifted his hand and inserted one finger into his nose before she even finished the thought. She giggled. His finger stayed there until she told him to drop it.

What do you want him to do, Christine?

"Pay attention to me," she said haltingly, uncertainly.

Satyr's mouth opened. More black ooze trickled out when he said, "So beautiful."

Christine smiled, her confidence building. "Do you…want me?"

Make him, Christine. Take control.

She pulled him closer and made him kiss her. The black ichor coating his mouth tasted like hazelnut. She moved her hands down to his belt buckle. If Karin was going to lose her virginity tonight, so would she. Maybe she would even be first. She glanced at the hands of her watch to mark the time.

She pulled his belt free and let it drop to the floor. The first time was supposed to hurt, and that used to make her afraid, but not anymore. She wondered if it would feel as good as the cut did. She wondered if anything could feel that good.

Turning her head, she caught a glimpse of herself in the cracked mirror: the shaved and dyed hair, the ring through her eyebrow.

"Tell me I look good," she said. "Tell me I look better than Karin."

Mom drains the last of her Passover wine, not bothering to dip her finger or put drops on her plate. She slams the glass down on the table so hard Christine thinks the stem might break. "Say it to my face, Matt! Come on, call me a bad mother to my face!"

Christine's heart pounds. She glances from Mom's red face to Dad's redder one.

"I'm not saying that," he insists. "It's just…well, look at her." He gestures at Christine. "How could you let her do that to herself?"

Christine, panicking, glances at Karin, but her no-longer-identical twin laughs, hiding her mouth behind her hand.

"Let her?" Mom snarls. "You think I want my daughter looking like a freak?"

Christine can't catch her breath. Everything was fine when they were dipping their pinkies in the wine. Why can't they go back to doing that?

"Don't call our daughter a freak," Dad says, loud enough for the neighbors to hear.

"Why not?" Karin asks, snickering. "That's what Alan called her in front of everyone at Spring Fling last night. He totally agrees with me that your haircut makes you look like a rugmuncher."

"Stop it!" Christine cries. She jumps to her feet, her chair scraping loudly on the floor, and runs from the table. It's a small apartment and the closest room is the bathroom. She locks herself in, slams down the toilet cover, and sits, trembling and scratching at the shapes moving under her skin.

"Oh, Christ," Dad says, his voice muffled by the door.

"Just ignore her," Karin says loudly, so Christine can hear. "It's all about attention with her. She's a huge drama queen."

Sliding closer to the door, Christine hears her parents mumbling to each other. Don't they care that she's locked herself in the bathroom? Why aren't they apologizing for the things they said about her? If it were Karin, they'd be kneeling by the door, begging forgiveness. But it's just Christine, the freak, the weaker twin, the second-born, so why bother?

Her father's voice floats softly through the door. "Shchin, boils."

They started again? Are they really dipping their pinkies in the wine and tapping them onto the plates like nothing happened, like her absence from the table doesn't mean anything?

"Barad, hail."

They're continuing without her like they don't even care. Maybe they never did. No one had expected her to survive anyway.

"Arbe, locusts."

Humiliation sticks to her like sweat. Her skin itches for the cut again, but she's left her bag in the other room. She doesn't have her pocketknife. She looks around the bathroom, opens the vanity under the sink. There, tucked behind a small leather travel bag, is the old fashioned shaving kit she gave Dad for Father's Day almost a year ago. The box is unopened; he never even used it. She tears it open and pulls out the safety razor. She twists the handle to open the metal top, then removes the double-edged blade.

Hello, Christine.

"Choshech," the voice on the other side of the door says. "Darkness."

This is all her fault. She stole your parents and tore them apart. She stole your boyfriend and turned him against you. Now it's time for you to take control, Christine. No one else will.

She holds the blade to her wrist. Something moves under the skin, bulging and rubbery.

Make her sorry for everything she's stolen from you, every name she called you.

She's so angry her hand trembles. She has trouble holding the razor steady.

"Makat bechoroth," her father's voice says. "The slaying of the first-born."

You can finally be free of her, Christine.

She presses the razor. It breaks her skin, stinging, and raises a dollop of blood on her wrist.

Do it. Show them all how perfect you are.

"In pain," she says, "I am perfection."

Show them you know how to take control.

She drags the razor down one wrist, then the other. It feels exquisite. As the blood starts to flow, she sees the eels coiled under her skin. Something's wrong. There are too many of them. They writhe and twist and fall out of her, one after another.

She's frightened, confused. This isn't like before. She opens the bathroom door. Blood seeps from the long gashes in her wrists. There's red all over her clothes, red all over the floor. She walks trembling into the dining room, arms held out. The others scream at the sight of her, springing back from the table, knocking over their chairs, as eel after slippery black eel drops from her wounds.

Her hip collides with the table, and she crumples onto it, knocking over the wine glasses. She's so drowsy, she just wants to close her eyes for a moment.

When she opens them again, a steaming carpet of eels writhes on the floor, hissing and snapping their powerful jaws. The lights flicker and dim. Eels have gotten into the wiring. She can see them coiled behind the walls like insulation.

A hand touches her back. Her mother, eyes a milky white, embraces her. "You were always our favorite, Christine," she says in a flat, dead voice. Black paste oozes from her mouth. "We hate Karin. Everything is her fault."

Her father, kneeling on the floor, repeatedly raises the carving knife and brings it down, sinking it into the bleeding pulp of Karin's chest. His face registers no emotion. "Makat bechoroth," he repeats, drooling black onto his shirt. "Makat bechoroth." The eels nip at the corpse's fingers and toes, tearing them from their sockets and fighting over the meat.

"Now we can all be happy again," her mother says.

"Doesn't feel like before," she murmurs weakly. "Did I cut too deep this time?"

"Shhhhh." Her mother strokes her hair. "You did just fine. You are perfection."

She can barely keep her eyes open. There's so much sticky red everywhere, and eels keep sliding out of the gashes in her arms. When will they stop? How many can there be?

In the dimming light, she watches the exodus pour out of her. Hundreds of them, thousands of them, going forth to a freedom that should have been hers.

MYSTERIES OF THE CURE

Not every story comes easily. In fact, most don't, at least not for me, but "Mysteries of the Cure" is a good example of one that went through a number of different versions before I got a handle on it. Originally, the story was even more surreal, had a completely different ending, and featured a cameo by the Devil. Go figure. But writing it helped me work through some lingering issues after my first marriage fell apart, and though it started off as a story about the deceptive, addictive healing power of sex, it took a while for it to finally make its true self known to me. It's really about heartbreak. (By the way, bonus points to anyone who correctly guesses where the names Justine and Eugenie come from.)

I can't find Justine. Her office Christmas party rages around me, all tinsel, carols and stupid hats. I'm desperate to leave, but I can't find her anywhere. A woman in a powder blue dress stands in front of the executive bathroom, grimacing and shifting impatiently from one foot to the other. She tells me Justine went in twenty minutes ago and still hasn't come out. Reaching for the knob, something tells me not to open that door. If I leave it alone, I can go on lying to myself for another eight years of marriage.

But I open the door and there she is, sitting on the marble sink with her skirt hiked up around her waist. Ryan Gupta, her partner in the Human Resources Department, is kneeling in front of her with his head between her thighs. He doesn't stop until Justine taps the top of his head and says, "I thought you locked the door."

Back home, we stare at each other in silence on the couch. I wait for an explanation, an apology, but Justine just looks at her hands. Finally she says, like she's been rehearsing the words, "I think it would be for the best if you moved out."

"Oh, that's rich," I say. "I catch you with another guy and you're telling me to move out?"

She looks at my face for a moment like she's trying to find something in me she still cares about, something that would make her change her mind. Then, evidently finding nothing, she says, "I think that would be for the best."

Just like that, with her voice remarkably calm for what she's saying, our marriage is over.

We started out as college sweethearts. I was Alpha Tau Omega, she was Alpha Omicron Pi. We met at a mixer and hit it off right away. Alpha and Alpha, we said. Two Alphas in a pod. We spent a lot of time in my narrow single bed in the ATO house, making love, tug-of-warring for the covers, asking each other stupid questions in the dark and laughing so loud my fraternity brothers would pound on the door and shout, "Fuck or sleep, choose one!"

These past couple of years, we hardly touched each other. One weekend a month, at best. The rest of the time, I'd rub myself with her sleeping next to me, hoping not to shake the mattress too much and wake her. It's painfully obvious now that we passed out expiration date long before I opened that bathroom door.

She stands up and says, "I'm going to bed. You can sleep here on the couch."

"And you can go fuck yourself," I say.

I watch her stomp to the bedroom and slam the door. Something snaps in my chest, jagged, hot and painful. I open my shirt and see a bumpy red rash over my heart. Great. My marriage is disintegrating *and* I've got hives. I slump back on the sofa and scan the apartment. Everything is steeped in the glow of memory. Here's the couch where we sat and watched our wedding video over and over again, poking fun at eccentric aunts and drunk, dancing cousins. There's the kitchen where we'd stand side by side, drinking wine and tenderizing cutlets while we discussed favorite names for the children we'd have one day. These things are dead now, waiting for the decay to come and erase every last trace of them.

My new apartment is in the same neighborhood, only a few blocks away from Justine. The floor is slanted, half the outlets don't work, the windows don't close right, and it's smaller than I'm used to. At first, I can't bring myself to unpack the few boxes I brought with me, as if this is all just temporary, Justine will call any minute and tell me she's broken it off with Ryan and could I possibly forgive her and please just come home. I would, too, even after her betrayal. I don't know how to be alone.

I can't sleep. My new bed is too big for one person. I roll and roll and never fall off, never bump into anyone. When I finally nod off, my sleep is constantly interrupted by the sound of crumbling granite. I wake up not knowing where I am.

My evenings are spent sitting in front of the television with a plastic tumbler of Johnny Walker Black. It's my liquid sleeping pill, the only thing that helps. Ice makes a different sound when dropped into a plastic cup—a desperate, utilitarian thump, not at all like the sharp clink it makes in the glassware we were given as a wedding present. But those glasses didn't come with me when I left. The plastic tumblers are from a discount store down the street.

Sighing, I put my feet up on a cardboard box marked *Living Room*, my makeshift coffee table until I can afford a real one, and shiver on the couch from the winter air sliding in around the loose window frames. I touch the radiator to see if it's on, and the metal breaks off in my hand, crisp and fragile like old papier-mâché.

The next morning, I wake up to see a long crack in the bedroom wall. Something black and oily oozes out of it, emitting a sweet, pungent odor like the dead rat we once found behind the refrigerator.

The rash on my chest is worse, and there's a festering sore on my right shin that's leaking dark liquid down my leg. It smells like whatever's coming out of the wall.

Justine works Saturday, and every Saturday around noon I used to treat myself to brunch alone at Harry's Luncheonette. I see no reason to change my routine now. Harry's is my spot, not hers. Eugenie is the waitress who always takes my order. She knows me by name and never bothers bringing me a menu, just asking if I want my usual. It makes me feel like I'm the only one who matters, and more than ever I need to feel that way again.

Sitting in my usual booth, I catch myself fiddling with the bare spot on my ring finger. I used to spin the gold wedding band with my thumb whenever I was nervous, often without even realizing it. Justine used to point it out to me all the time. I'm surprised to find myself still doing it, spinning that phantom ring and watching Eugenie walk toward me with a warm grin, her dark blonde hair bouncing at her shoulders.

Another waitress comes up behind me, a curly-haired old woman I've never seen before. She pulls out her notepad and taps a pen against it. "What'll it be, mister?"

"I got him," Eugenie says, hurrying over and shooing the old woman away. Then she turns to me and flashes a grin. "Where've you been hiding? You didn't come in last week. I was worried about you."

"It's been a tough couple of weeks," I say.

She must see it in my face because she puts a hand on my shoulder and says, "I thought something was up. I'm good at figuring things out like that. You okay?"

She has a kind face, bright eyes and a smile that would make any man want her. A great sense of humor, too. The kind of woman who makes you sad to be married. On those nights when Justine wouldn't touch me, Eugenie was the one I fantasized about most. I've wondered many times what it would be like to be with her.

And now, suddenly, I'm free to find out. It's not like there's anything stopping me anymore. I haven't asked someone out in the better part of a decade. It takes me a moment to remember how.

"Huh," Eugenie replies. "For some reason, I thought you were married. Didn't you bring someone in here before?"

I show her my hand. No wedding ring.

She smiles that gorgeous smile, her sparkling eyes almost disappearing in her cheeks. "Yeah, sure," she says. "Why not?" She laughs a nervous, embarrassed, delightful laugh.

Watching her walk away from my table, the way her ass fills out the back of her jeans, the way her hips swing with each step, something stirs inside me, something so absent from my life with Justine I almost don't recognize it. I have to cross my legs to hide the erection straining against my fly.

I catch myself spinning the phantom wedding ring again and find a new black sore on the back of my hand.

I spot Justine on the street after leaving Harry's. Why isn't she at work? It's only been two weeks since I moved out, much too soon to see her again. I try to turn away before she notices me, but she calls my name.

"I didn't see you," I say. It's a pathetic lie, and I'm sure she sees through it. "How've you been?"

"Are you coming from Harry's?" she asks, smirking. "I guess some things never change."

"Guess not," I say.

"How's your new apartment?"

"Perfect," I lie again. The sore on my left hand itches under the lambskin glove, but I refuse to scratch it. I can't afford any signs of weakness, not in front of her. A rictus smile is frozen on my face. My nose drips from the cold air. The glove fills with warm, thick liquid.

She looks down at her shoes like she's mulling something over, then says, "Ryan is moving in."

Ryan, with his face buried between her legs, his hands moving up her thighs. I force the image out of my head. "Already? That was quick." I don't know what else to say.

She keeps her eyes on her shoes. "I want you to know I never intended to fall in love with someone else. I never meant to hurt you."

"But it happened just the same, didn't it?" Then the implication of her words sinks in. "How long has it been going on?" Maybe that's why she's not at work. Maybe she never really worked Saturdays.

Justine sucks her teeth and glares at me like it's none of my business how long she's been screwing someone behind my back. "Look," she says, "he needs closet space, so do you want the things you left or should I just throw them out?"

"Oh, fuck you," I say, walking away.

She calls after me, "He's everything you're not."

Alpha and Alpha. Two Alphas in a pod. Jesus.

Back at my apartment, the heat still isn't working. One of the windows slid open while I was out, and a chill wind blows through my living room. Closing the window again, I notice its frame is no longer white-painted wood. It's bone, mossy and slick. My fingers come away sticky.

Eugenie spends most of our dinner date telling me about the men she's been with in the past, how all of them were jerks who used her and dumped her when they got bored.

"Sounds like my ex," I say. I tell her about the separation without saying too much about Justine. I don't want to talk about her. Invoking her name is like having her at the table with us.

Eugenie shows compassion in all the right spots, nodding or shaking her head along with me. I can tell she understands what I'm going through. We've both been hurt. There's a bond between the walking wounded.

Desperate not to spend another night alone, I pour on the charm over dessert, really working the seduction. I'm surprised I still have it in me after all these years. I catch my reflection in the wine glass. The skin under my right eye is broken, turning black at the edges. The stark white crest of my cheekbone juts through. When I reach for the glass, I find the sore on the back of my hand has gotten worse. It's grown wider, split open, and I can see the tendons and muscles inside.

The top two buttons of Eugenie's black blouse are undone. When she leans forward to take my festering hand in hers, I get a clear view of her cleavage. "I'd love to see your new place," she says. "Maybe we can pick up a bottle of wine on the way."

They say everyone kisses differently. My first kiss was with Liz

Parker in eighth grade. She kept her lips hard and flicked her tongue on mine with all the gentleness of a motorized fan rotor. Barbara Jakubowski, my girlfriend through most of high school, kissed like a puppy, licking my lips and face until I looked like I'd just stepped from the shower. Justine gave tight pecks, rarely using her tongue. Most of the time she was worried about mussing her lipstick, even after the minister said, "You may kiss the bride."

Eugenie, by contrast, keeps her mouth open and relaxed, her lips loose, her tongue unafraid of mine. We embrace on my couch, her fingers roaming over my chest and stomach. I move one hand slowly up her smooth silk blouse until I feel the mound of her breast under my palm. She doesn't push me away.

"Let's go in the other room," she says.

We're everywhere in the hours that follow: on the bedroom floor, on the desk against the wall, and finally on the bed itself. Eugenie has a belly button ring and a blue and white butterfly tattoo on her ass that covers the name of an old lover. I can hear her heart beating in my head.

Running sores and coagulated black goo cover my naked body. The stench of decay is overpowering. The crack in the wall tears wider, longer, extending onto the ceiling and dripping its syrupy ooze all over us like rain.

"Oh yes!" Eugenie cries. "Oh God!"

Her heartbeat is deafening.

I'm surprised how difficult it is sleeping with someone next to me. I guess I'm not used to it anymore. I try to roll away from her, get some space to breathe, but she follows me, wrapping her arms around me, keeping me trapped. I can't sleep until I'm all the way on the other side of the bed from her.

In the morning, she blinks sleepily at me and looks at the clock. "My shift starts soon. Is it okay if I shower here?"

She doesn't wait for me to answer before she rolls out of bed. A piece of the sheet sticks to her back, pulling like taffy before it tears off the mattress. It leaves a wet sucking wound by the pillow. Red and pulsating.

"I can't wait for you to meet my friend Megan," she says,

walking naked toward the bathroom. Her body looks different now. Bulkier, looser. Used. "You two'll get along so well. She has the same sense of humor you do. We should all get together sometime."

I get out of bed, pull on my boxer shorts and open the closet, catching my reflection in the mirror on the back of the door. The sore on my right cheek has healed. The ones on my hand and leg, too. The decay is gone. I turn and look at the bed, with its rumpled sheets and a towel covering the wet spot. Was that what cured me? It's fitting, in a way.

Justine fucked someone else. Now I have, too. I hope wherever she is, whatever she's doing, she feels that. I hope it hurts her.

The shower running in the bathroom sounds like heavy nails dropping into a metal bucket. It's driving me crazy. I can't wait for Eugenie to leave.

But the cure doesn't last. The sores come back.

I don't want to meet Eugenie's friend Megan. I don't want to meet her parents, her movie club, her brother, her cat. I just want the cure. That's all. But Eugenie wants more. She wants us to do things together, go to movies and dinner and hang out with her friends. She gives me the cure less and less.

I watch other women on the street or in the halls of my office and wonder if they might be better sources for the cure. Sitting with Eugenie in Dobb's Pub one night, I look past her shoulder at four women playing doubles at the pool table. I hear their hearts beating almost in unison. Any of them could cure me. It doesn't have to be Eugenie.

Three weeks after our first date, she comes over but doesn't want to have sex. She says she's exhausted and just wants to sleep. It's clear this isn't working out. It's time to find another source. As far as I'm concerned, she can't leave fast enough in the morning.

Eugenie calls me from Harry's while she's on break the next night. "You never seem to be interested in anything but sex. I need to know I'm more than just a fuck buddy to you."

"I'm on my way out the door," I say. I take a sip of scotch in my pajamas and make sure the TV's on mute. "I can't really talk about this now. Maybe later?"

I really don't want to have that discussion. All I want is for Eugenie to come over, cure me and leave in the morning, but obviously that's never going to happen again. So what's the point? I start screening my calls and erasing the messages as soon as I hear her voice.

Without access to the cure, the decay comes back fast, worse than before. Examining the sore on my cheek in the bathroom mirror, I find the skin has dissolved away and even more of the bone is poking through. My hands, my legs, all the leaking wounds have returned. New ones, too, on my stomach and sides. I need the cure, but calling Eugenie is out of the question. She won't give it to me. She'll just want to talk about our relationship. I grab the bottle of scotch and sit down on a couch made of slimy brown animal bones and leathery skin stretched tight. A hollow box of stiff, puckered meat squats where the television used to be. I flip through the channels, but each one is showing the same thing: a big, beating heart.

Eugenie catches me a few days later in a rare moment when I forget to screen my calls. I pick up the handset, a fusion of chicken bones with human teeth for dialing buttons, and push aside the dangling fatty skin over the receiver so I can hear.

"I know you've been avoiding me," she says, her voice thick with anger. "I told you I'm good at figuring things out. I'll save you the trouble of having to be man enough to confront me about it. I thought you were different, but you're not. You used me just like they did. I can't *believe* I let my guard down. I'm such a fool. I can't believe I actually let myself develop feelings for you."

A long strip of skin, gummy and edged with a sickly black, sloughs off my arm and lies next to the phone like an awkward silence.

"I need more than this," she says. "And you shouldn't be getting involved with anyone right now. You're obviously not ready to act like an adult in a relationship."

"I didn't ask for your advice," I say. "You have no idea what I'm going through. If you're looking for someone who'll do whatever you want, get a fucking dog."

I hear her heart break over the phone. It sounds like a pencil snapping in half. Justine broke my heart, and now I've broken someone else's. I hope it stings her to know what she's turned me into.

"Don't come back to Harry's anymore," Eugenie says, her voice soft and low. "I don't want to see you there."

When I slam the handset back on its cradle, I see the bones of my fingers piercing through the skin.

The bike messenger standing between the cubicles of my office can't be more than twenty years old. He has a ring through his nose and dreadlocks coming out from under his helmet. He hands me a big envelope and says, "Package for you, bro." My coworkers look up from their work, happy for the distraction. I sign for it, then tear the envelope open. My breath catches in my throat. Justine has served me with divorce papers. Right in front of everyone. And my coworkers know it, too. They can see it in my face. The ones standing near me back away, as if they can sense the decay spreading from my body and infecting everything I touch.

A bubbling sore ruptures on my palm. Beneath my shirt, I feel two ribs puncture the fragile, moldering skin of my side. I have to find a new source for the cure, before I rot away to nothing.

I hear a heartbeat behind me and turn. Betty Morlan from Accounts Payable walks by. She's divorced, too, and she's always complaining that she can't get laid anymore, too old at forty and too thick around the middle. I take a step toward her, but she sees something in my eyes, something predatory, and hurries away.

The subway that takes me home is the elongated ribcage of a massive serpent, the ribs sharp and slick with a brown jelly. A small woman with big eyes sits across from me. We make eye contact, but I glance away, unsure what to do. She looks young, maybe college-aged, maybe fresh out. Her heart beats strong and steady in my head. The need for the cure thunders through my body in time with her pulse.

She gets off at the next stop. The rot on my face feels worse. I can touch my teeth through the hole in my cheek. How much time do I have left? I should've followed her off the train. *Taken* the cure from her if she wouldn't give it freely.

I get out at my stop and walk home. I can hear the heartbeat of every woman I pass on the sidewalk drumming in my skull, loud, incessant. It's driving me mad.

Lying in bed, thick chunks of skin sliding off my bones, I stare up at the crack in the ceiling. It's grown even longer, wider, and inside, where I'd expect to see support beams and insulation, there's only a deep blackness. Little white flakes emerge from the blackness and drift lazily down toward me. Snow. I hear something, too. It's faint, but as it grows louder it becomes a rhythm I recognize. A heartbeat. Calling me. I stand up on the mattress. Cold air breezes out of the crack. If I stretch, I can reach the edge. I grab hold, hoist myself up and inside.

And suddenly I'm standing in a brick alleyway, shivering against the cold and the night's softly falling snow. It takes me a moment to realize where I am. The alley outside Dobb's Pub. What am I doing here?

At the end of the alley, women walk in and out the pub's door. I've been given one last chance at the cure. Looking down at myself, I see only chalky bones held together by stringy black tendons and a few patches of raw, seeping flesh. I have very little time left. So what am I supposed to do, just grab someone and pull her into the alley? That's insane. And yet, I've been without the cure for too long. If I let it slip away again, there will be nothing left at all. What choice do I have?

I slink back into the shadows to watch without being seen. I don't know how to do this. There are too many couples. I should wait for a woman who's alone.

Then I see her. A woman with long dark hair leaves the bar and stands outside, right by the mouth of the alley. She tries to light her cigarette, but the wind keeps blowing out her lighter flame. She's by herself. I take a step forward. I'm shaking all over. I have no idea what I'm doing. What if I screw up? What if she gets away? I could rot into a big black stain on the ground before I get another chance.

The walls around me shudder and buck. A long crack tears through one, raining pieces of cement and brick dust onto the snow. She's still playing with her lighter, not moving from her spot. I lunge for her. I mean to cover her mouth, but I'm clumsy and nervous. I grab the back of her coat collar instead and pull. She shrieks, drops the cigarette and lighter. The pub door opens and a tall, muscular man saunters out onto the sidewalk.

"Claire, where are—?"

Dammit, she's not alone after all. She shrieks again as I pull her into the dark of the alley. He hears her, runs into the alley, pushes me up against the bricks just as I get one hand over her mouth and another around her neck.

"What the fuck do you think you're doing?" he shouts in my face, but all I can hear is the rapid-fire beating of the woman's heart. "Let go of her, asshole!" But I refuse to let go, even when he punches me in the stomach. I can't lose the cure again. I can't.

The crack in the alley wall is visible over his shoulder. A pale hand reaches out slowly from inside, wrapping its long fingers around the edge. The shape that pulls itself out of the crack is momentarily blocked by the man's head as he continues yelling and punching. When he moves to try to loosen my grip on his girlfriend's throat, I finally see her.

Eugenie.

"I don't understand," I say.

"It's easy," the man replies. "You let go of her or I beat the shit out of you. What's not to fucking understand?" He hits me in the stomach again, but there's so little of me left it doesn't even register.

Eugenie moves behind him. She's changed so much. Where once she had a kind face, with a warm smile and eyes that disappeared in her cheeks when she laughed, there's now only mottled skin sagging off her bones. Her sores drip black slime down her clothes. A bleeding red wound puckers on her chest where her heart used to be.

Oh God. I infected her. I gave her my decay.

She grabs the man off me and pulls him away, one hand

over his mouth. His eyes widen in alarm. I pull the woman closer to me, keeping her mouth covered so she won't scream. The four of us stand in the dark of the alley, looking at each other, waiting.

Eugenie smiles at me. It's a cruel smile, and her teeth are tiny bone daggers. Her eyes are black pools. Is that what I look like, too? Is that what I've become? I glance down and see a red, puckered hole in my chest, just like hers. There's no heart inside. There hasn't been since the moment I opened that bathroom door at Justine's office party. She took mine. I took Eugenie's. That's how the disease spreads.

Eugenie holds one claw-like hand in front of the terrified man's eyes. Then she sinks her fingers effortlessly through his coat, his shirt, and into his chest. He spasms, spits geysers of blood from his mouth.

"I figured it out," she says. "The cure lasts longer if you take it right from the heart." She pulls the beating organ from his chest, licks her rotting lips.

I look at my hand, my bone-sharp fingers. I look at the woman. Her eyes are wide, frightened. She tries to shake her head. I hear her heart thumping like a homing beacon. All I have to do is take it. The alternative… No, there is no alternative.

I lock eyes with Eugenie. She nods. There's a bond between the walking wounded.

Together, we take our cures.

STREET CRED

"Street Cred" first appeared in an anthology that was published on CD-ROM, back when that was considered cutting edge. (Although I have to admit it was cool to be in an anthology that came with its own theme song!) When it was later reprinted in my first collection, Walk In Shadows, it became one of the most popular stories in the book. "Street Cred" is a lot more hardcore than what I usually write. It's gross. The characters are despicable and say stupid things. But in a story about dehumanization, about treating people like things, I suppose you have to have characters doing awful stuff. And zombies, of course. The Brooklyn neighborhood where Richie and the gang live is where I was living at the time, but the garage on the corner of Atlantic and Court is long gone. Now it's a luxury apartment building with a bank, a shoe store, and a yogurt and smoothie shop on its ground floor. The tide of gentrification marches forward as relentlessly as any zombie horde.

They were the last of the Nevins Street Necro Fiends. The rest were either in jail or had bailed like pussies. So it was down to the Hardcore Four: Deadbeat, Rotgut, big deaf Thorazine Joe, and Saw Boy.

Then there was Richie Swerdlow, also known as Ace.

Ace wasn't legit yet. He hadn't been officially initiated into the gang, but he got to hang out with them at school, and once Deadbeat had even called him an honorary Necro Fiend. Honorary was better than nothing, he figured, and it still carried weight. With his new reputation, all the trouble at school disappeared. The glares of contempt he got by the lockers were changing to looks of respect, maybe even fear. Big Louis stopped shoving him around on the schoolyard basketball court. Ace was pretty sure some of the girls were checking him out now, too. Even Shaniqua, with her long braids and gold tooth and killer body, had smiled at him once in study hall. He'd seen it clear as day: she looked past the three desks between them like they weren't even there and smiled her golden smile. Right at him.

He replayed the moment in his head every day. Shaniqua was fine. No, she was more than fine, she was untouchable to the likes of him. But that day she had looked at him differently. Smiled like he wasn't just another pathetic white boy trying to fit in at P.S. 38 in Brooklyn.

There was a name for it, a media buzzword. He heard it all the time when rock stars got caught with guns at the airport, or when rappers and movie stars got in public fistfights with drunk assholes who thought they could talk trash.

Street cred.

Being a Necro Fiend—a legit member, not just honorary— would give him that. It would put an end to the taunting and bullying, the rat-tails in the gym locker room, the *Move your ass, white boy!* It would make him more than just a single white dot floating in a public school sea of brown and black. Street cred. He wanted it more than anything he'd ever wanted in his life. He needed it if he was going to survive high school.

The Necro Fiends teased him, too, sometimes, but they were the only friends he had at school. He couldn't afford to lose them. Not now, not when acceptance, even respect, was so close he could almost grasp it.

Not now that Shaniqua had *smiled* at him.

The Nevins Street Necro Fiends were all Hispanic, and sometimes Ace worried that his pinkish pale complexion and the stupid feathery eyelashes he'd gotten from his mother would hold him back, that maybe they'd never make him a real gang member after all. Maybe they just kept him around as a joke, all *Check out this loser white boy following us around*, but it was never really like that. He asked all the time when they would make him legit, and they always said, "Soon, *hermano,* but you can't rush it."

He believed them, because sometimes they let him tag along for target practice. That's what they called it when they went looking for zombies to shoot. Five years after the Reanimation Crisis emptied the graves, there were still a few of those nasty dirtwalkers lurking around. Even the Army riflemen and the trained professionals of the local Body Retrieval Units couldn't get every last one of them. They were getting harder to find these days, especially with the new government regulations about death and burial being strictly enforced, but the dirtwalkers were out there. You just had to know where to look.

Haitian neighborhoods were the best bet for target practice. For years there'd been a problem with the Haitians hiding their dead family members and tending to them like they were still alive. Still funny Uncle Bruce or sweet Aunt Mary instead of the hungry walking corpses they really were. Break into any project basement and you'd probably find half a dozen dirtwalkers huddling in the dark corners, eating the raw meals their families left for them, their faces smeared with chicken blood, little white feathers stuck to their fingers. Easy pickings. A bullet to the brain, and down they went.

Ace was okay with a gun, but the others were better. They'd been doing it longer. Target practice, plowing, it was all part of what Deadbeat called the horror show.

The first time he heard about plowing, it made his stomach spaz out. Rotgut told him about the zombie chick he caught in an alley one night; he could tell it'd been a real hottie when it was alive, all tits and ass, and it wasn't too fucked up yet from being dead. He chopped off its arms, tore open its dress and plowed her good; really got his rocks off, he said.

"Plowing," Rotgut said, "is what makes you a real Necro Fiend. Any idiot with a gun can off a dirtwalker. But how many have the balls to fuck one, huh?" He slapped Ace on the back. "Your turn will come soon, don't worry."

Later, back home, Ace threw up and couldn't close his eyes all night. But now way was he going to be known as the white boy who was too much of a pussy to keep partying, so the next day he acted like everything was cool. He put up with their jibes and snaps and kept his mouth shut. True Necro Fiends weren't pussies. True Necro Fiends didn't bail.

Ace's family owned a brownstone right on the corner of Dean and Nevins. His bedroom on the second floor overlooked the street. The sun was just beginning to set when he heard Deadbeat calling up to him. Ace frowned. Something wasn't right. They always waited until dark before going out, and they always told him when to be ready. They hadn't said they were coming by. He threw on his jacket, crawled out the window onto the rusty brown fire escape and scurried down the ladder.

He dropped onto the sidewalk in front of Deadbeat, and said, "What's up?"

Deadbeat was the leader, no questions asked. He had the coolest black leather jacket, made even cooler by the Necro Fiends tag on the back: a skeleton of painted white lines, and between its legs, a third line, poking straight out. Wearing gang tags at school was supposed to get you an immediate suspension, but Deadbeat wore his jacket every day and nothing ever happened. The administration didn't give a shit about anything anymore.

Deadbeat, the Big Boss, was tall for his age—fifteen, like Ace—with slick black hair and a peach-fuzz mustache shading his upper lip. Ace still couldn't muster up any acceptable facial hair. Dressed in old, torn jeans and an Ozzy t-shirt, he wished he could look as cool as Deadbeat looked in his black leather jacket and maroon velour pants.

Rotgut was shorter than Deadbeat, with a pimply brown face and the start of a fuzzy soul patch under his lower lip. He wore the same beat up denim jacket and creased leather pants he always wore. If he owned any other clothes, Ace never saw them. Rotgut was also a big-time prick, but Ace never had to give him face because Rotgut was second in command after Deadbeat.

Thorazine Joe was Deadbeat's lumbering deaf brother, a real retard-case that drove everyone crazy, but no one, especially Ace, was going to say anything to Deadbeat about it. Right of blood protected the big freak, though Deadbeat didn't seem to mind his brother's gang nickname, even if Joe had stopped taking his meds long ago and now sold them to the junkies at school instead. Thorazine Joe stood there in his sweats, looking in the other direction, and wearing those stupid earphones he always wore. They weren't even plugged into anything—that would be a waste of music—but he wore them anyway, as if to hide the fact that he was deaf.

Ace saw the long handle of a wooden baseball bat poking out of the top of Thorazine Joe's blue backpack, and right away he knew what that meant. Joe only brought the Louisville Slugger along for target practice. He preferred it to a gun. Retard.

"Thought we'd go for a little stroll," Deadbeat said.

Ace straightened up. He wished he were taller. "Yeah?"

"Yeah," Rotgut said, scratching the new hair on his chin. "Saw Boy's waiting for us over at Deadbeat's place."

Ace turned to Deadbeat. "I didn't know we were doing anything tonight."

Deadbeat smiled, showing the solid gold tooth in the front of his mouth. It wasn't as nice as the one Shaniqua flashed at Ace in study hall, but it sure was cool.

"Consider it a Halloween surprise," Deadbeat said. "The party's just waiting for us, *hermano*."

"What's the matter, Iron Man?" Rotgut said, poking Ace's Ozzy t-shirt. "You pussying out? Too many niggas in one place for you, *Swerdlow*?"

"Fuck you, Rotgut. I'm called Ace now, got it?" He turned back to Deadbeat. "What's the plan?"

"Party doesn't start until we get there," Deadbeat said. "Tonight's gonna be a real horror show. Big time."

Thorazine Joe turned to face them and signed something at Deadbeat, all the while smiling that retard smile of his.

Rotgut tapped Joe on the arm and said, "You gotta learn to talk, man. Wiggling your fat-ass fingers like that, you look all gay and shit." Joe signed again. Rotgut looked at Deadbeat. "The fuck is he saying now?"

Deadbeat pulled a black handgun from the back of his belt, all nonchalant like the time he dissed Mr. Bersa right to his pasty white face in gym class, and popped the magazine out of the butt to check if it was loaded. "You talking about my brother, Rotgut?" he asked.

Deadbeat didn't need to check the gun. Of course it was loaded. Even if Ace couldn't see the copper gleam of the top bullet's casing, he knew Deadbeat never carried an empty gun. He was just doing it to psych Rotgut out.

Rotgut backed down like he always did, clowning around and saying he was just fooling. Ace hoped someday Deadbeat would shoot that prick anyway.

He looked at the gun in Deadbeat's hand. The grooved grip and the etched logo on the side of the barrel tagged it as one of the new Glock 36 autos. The extended magazine made it a seven-rounder. A police gun.

Ace tensed up, wondering if Deadbeat had done something stupid to get ahold of a police gun, but then he remembered Deadbeat's uncle was a cop. He probably stole it from his uncle's closet or something. No biggie.

Ace knew a lot about guns. Everybody did, ever since the gun laws were changed because of the Reanimation Crisis. *Guns Illustrated* became a government-sponsored newsletter, sent to every citizen's home on a monthly basis, and while owning a firearm was still not considered mandatory, household tax credits were given for each gun purchased. The President said owning a gun was tantamount to helping the government rid the country of zombies; the more guns you bought, the more you were helping. It pissed him off that his dad wouldn't let him have a gun of his own yet. There were only two in the house: a SIG Arms Pro 2009 handgun in his parents' bedroom, and a wicked cool Browning Mark 2 Safari autoloading rifle that he *never* got to touch.

He dad just didn't get it. He said Ace was too young to have his own gun, or to handle the ones they owned. It was always the same thing. He used words like "dangerous" and "accident" a lot, but by then Ace usually tuned him out. It was like his dad had never seen the commercial that was always on TV.

A small child sitting on a couch, not more than six years old, looking directly into the camera as someone, unseen, asks him questions.

"Do you know where your daddy's gun is?"

The boy nods.

"Did he teach you how to use it?"

"Uh huh."

"And what would you do if you ever saw a zombie?"

The child raises his hand, his index finger and thumb extending to simulate a pistol. He points it at the camera and says, "Bang!"

The screen goes black, and then the name Wiltshire Weapons Training appears in white, along with a phone number.

"Wiltshire Weapons Training," a soothing voice says. "It's never too soon to start learning."

"Joe wants to know if we're going, or what?" Deadbeat said, reading his brother's hands.

"Yeah, we're going," Rotgut said, slapping Ace on the arm. "Right, *Ace*?" He put a mocking emphasis on the name, but his beady eyes said, *Swerdlow.*

Big-time prick.

"Sure," Ace said. "My parents won't know I'm gone until dinner."

The words had come out of his mouth like a train with no brakes. He heard himself say it and immediately knew it was a mistake. Deadbeat and Rotgut laughed, and Thorazine Joe signed furiously, wanting to know what was so funny.

"Mama Swerdlow's boy may or may not be back in time for dinner," Rotgut said. "Who gives a shit?"

Ace let it roll off his back. He was a Necro Fiend, or almost one. He *belonged*. If Rotgut didn't like it, he could go fuck himself.

Deadbeat lifted the back of his shirt and put the Glock away. "You got a piece yet?" he asked Ace.

"No," Ace said. "Not yet. They won't let me have one until I'm sixteen." It was a lie, a simple switching of numbers, sixteen instead of eighteen, but it made him feel better, and it didn't make him look like a pussy in front of them.

"Your parents suck," Deadbeat said. "What, do they *like* paying taxes?"

"Can you lend me one?" Ace asked.

"We'll see." Deadbeat led them down Nevins Street, past the rows of townhouses and brownstones that lined the road.

Ace kept his eyes down, looking at the concrete steps of the tall stoops and the trees planted at intervals in the sidewalk. This was his neighborhood, and it embarrassed him that it was so much fancier than theirs. They probably thought he was a rich, spoiled brat, but he'd show them. He was as tough as they were. As tough as anyone.

A bored Army private was stationed on the next corner. Ace could tell he hadn't seen a zombie in weeks. His eyes were practically begging for a stray dirtwalker to come shuffling down Bergen Street so he could shoot it in the head and have something to tell his friends for once.

"How's it going," the private said when he saw them. "Don't forget, curfew is earlier tonight. Ten o'clock, on account of Halloween. Be safe, all right?"

"Uh huh," Deadbeat said, and they kept walking. "I don't know if I'm in the mood for plowing today," he continued. It was something only Deadbeat could say. He called the shots. If anyone else said it, everyone would call him a pussy and then there would definitely be plowing no matter what. "I got too much pussy at that party last night. My Johnson ain't ready for more yet. Maybe just a little target practice." He made his hand into a gun, aimed with one eye down the street, and said, "Pow!"

Behind him, Thorazine Joe mimicked his older brother and laughed his retard laugh. Rotgut laughed, too, and Ace thought he'd better laugh or something might happen—they might call him *pussy* or *Swerdlow* again—so he laughed and said, "Sounds good to me."

"You don't got no piece yet," Deadbeat reminded him. "Maybe we'll do the shooting, and you can do the plowing, huh?"

"Whatever," Ace said. He kept the smile on his face, and shrugged all nonchalant, like Deadbeat did when Ms. Morales, the homeroom teacher, gave him a detention for saying *puta* in class. Deadbeat was the coolest. Nothing mattered to him, so nothing mattered to Ace, either. Necro Fiends didn't give a shit about anything but messing with dirtwalkers.

"They're not dirtwalkers, they're zombies," Saw Boy said. He scratched at the darkening mustache on his pale mocha lip. He had a weird scar on his right eyebrow that Ace had never worked up the nerve to ask about.

The five of them sat in a rough circle on the worn orange-brown carpet in Deadbeat's drab basement, passing around a sweet-smelling joint.

"What are you talking about?" Ace said. The tip of the rolling paper burned into glowing curls.

"That's the truth," Saw Boy said. His eyes were rimmed with red. "Officially, they're reanimates. That's what they call them on the news. Sometimes they call them zombies. But dirtwalker is slang. It's a bad word, like spic or chink or whatever."

Rotgut laughed. "They don't got no feelings, dickwad."

Ace laughed, too. Maybe Saw Boy didn't want to hurt the zombies' feelings, but he had no problem cutting them to pieces with his father's Craftsman sixteen-inch chainsaw.

What a beauty that thing was: shiny red body, black grip bar across the top covered with a comfortable foam wrap, and when it roared to life it sounded like Hell coming for you on a Harley. Saw Boy's dad never even went into his workshop anymore, so Saw Boy never got caught taking it out. Gas wasn't a problem, either. The neglected workshop was stacked with jugs of it. It was Saw Boy's paradise.

"Come on," Deadbeat said. "They're fucking *dead*. We can do whatever we want to them."

"They're not human," Rotgut agreed. "Not anymore, anyway. So who gives a shit? If it wasn't for us, there'd be plenty more of those dirtwalkers—oh, excuse me, I mean *reanimates*— all over the damn place. They're a menace. They kill people. They *eat* people. You ask me, society *owes* us for picking them off."

Saw Boy took a long drag off the joint, and when he spoke clouds came out of his mouth. "I ain't arguing with you. Just telling you how some people see it."

"Some people can kiss my still-living ass," Rotgut said, slapping the back of his leather pants.

Bored, Ace turned to the pile of titty mags on the dusty

carpet near him. He grabbed the top one and dragged it onto his lap. He flipped it open to the middle. The featured model was some chick named Lavender St. John. Ace thought his jeans were going to bust. Her tits were round and big, like perfect flesh-colored oranges, with juicy pink nipples poking out.

Just like the women on the Web pages his mother caught him looking at before she took away his Internet access. She told him most women didn't look like that, but Ace knew the first girl he did it with would have a body to die for. Like Shaniqua, with her ass filling the back of her tight jeans and her sweater straining and stretching over her curves.

"Check out the perv," Rotgut said, poking Ace in the arm. "Why don't you try to keep it in your pants?"

"Blow me," Ace said.

"You talking to me, or the girl?" Rotgut howled like a wolf.

Ace looked back down at the glossy photo spread.

Lavender St. John's face elongated suddenly, the flesh pulling along her cheeks and melting around her eyes into long, gooey, pink strands.

"What the fuck?"

Her breasts swelled, and her nipples opened into fiery red eyes. Something was snaking out of the patch of hair between her legs, something Ace didn't want to see.

He tossed the magazine away. "Fuck!"

Saw Boy laughed. "Forgot to tell you. I laced the weed with a little something extra, on account of it being such a special night."

Then Saw Boy's arm stretched all the way up the stairs and slammed a door somewhere in the house.

"Shit," Deadbeat said, glancing up at the ceiling. "We should get going before they come back. If my old man's been hitting the bottle again…"

The magazine bulged and flapped on the floor where it fell. Lavender St. John pulled herself out, naked and glistening, her mouth stretching into an enormous toothy cave, big enough to bite off Ace's head. He nearly peed his pants. Then she was gone, and the magazine lay motionless on the floor.

"Show time," Rotgut said.

And then they were outside, making their way up Atlantic Avenue in the dark, trying not to get caught after curfew. For a moment, Ace thought he saw Lavender St. John emerge from the darkness, coming to get him with her eyeball breasts and the thing snaking out of her crotch, but it was just a lamppost.

"Shouldn't have laced it," Ace said, but no one heard, so maybe he didn't say it, maybe he only thought it, maybe they were still in Deadbeat's basement and Saw Boy wasn't carrying his chainsaw and Thorazine Joe wasn't carrying his bat and the others weren't carrying handguns while his own hands were empty, maybe they weren't heading up Atlantic Avenue in the dead of night on Halloween, the one night when there would be extra military and police presence on the streets to keep boys like them from making trouble.

They ducked into the alley next to a bike shop while two police officers clip-clopped past them on horseback. The horses had skull heads and twitching serpent ears. Ace blinked his eyes until the horses looked right again.

Saw Boy murmured something about the garage, and then they were there, suddenly, on the corner of Court and Atlantic: the four-level garage that covered half the block like a huge, oatmeal-brown cement box. Behind them, the busiest intersection in downtown Brooklyn during the day was now as empty as a ghost town.

"We're here tonight to honor the newest member of the Nevins Street Necro Fiends," Deadbeat said. They passed through the green metal turnstile into the garage. "That's you, Ace."

"Holy shit!" Ace said. "For real?"

Deadbeat nodded. "After tonight, you'll be legit. But there's something you have to do first, something we all did to become members."

Next to him, Rotgut stuck a finger from one hand into a circle he made with the other. "Tonight's your big night."

Ace looked at his own hands. They were ten feet long, and his pale fingers stretched to touch the cars along the far wall.

Thorazine Joe grabbed Ace by his jacket collar and, all of them laughing, pulled him along to the cement stairway at the side of the garage, then down into darkness.

Down to where the air stank of oil, rust and rotting flesh.

The drug opened up like a blossom in his bloodstream. Everything merged into a single image, a single stretching moment in Ace's head:

Dark ragged shapes came out of the black corners of the underground level, human but different, some just skeletons with strips of tattered flesh hanging off their bones, others newly dead, weaving slowly between the abandoned cars, walking stiffly or dragging themselves along the ground because their legs were gone, and then the sound of Saw Boy's chainsaw starting up, carving through them—the pitch got higher when it hit bone, Ace noticed—and there were gunshots and the hollow *clonk* of a wooden bat, and Ace screamed or maybe he laughed as he watched it all happen, and then there was only one zombie left, female, and Thorazine Joe Louisville-slugged it until it stopped fighting, and then Deadbeat and Rotgut grabbed its arms and held it down on the hood of an old red Chevy while Joe clapped and hollered like a retard and jumped up and down, and Saw Boy put his chainsaw down and held one of its legs, and Ace was on top of it, and they were chanting his name and laughing and Saw Boy gave Thorazine Joe a high five, and the whole side of the dirtwalker's head had been royally fucked up, gashed and looking like raw meat, obliterating half its mane of crusted blonde hair, and it kept trying to bite him with its moldy teeth, and there was an awful gangrenous rot around its crotch where Saw Boy lifted up the shredded remains of its dress, and over Rotgut's shoulder Ace saw a human ribcage lying on the floor all red and white like something from a butcher's shop, and somehow Ace's fly was already down, and the dirtwalker was cold and dry where he touched it, cold and dry on the inside, and Ace thought its green wrinkled face looked angry because of what he was doing, but that didn't make sense because everyone knew dirtwalkers didn't have feelings, they weren't even human, not anymore, they were less than human, he could do whatever he wanted to them, and the guys were all hollering his name and clapping and jumping up and down and chanting "Plow it, plow it," and Ace's stomach hurt and his throat shuddered, and the zombie's moldering face was covered in vomit though he didn't remember actually puking, and he couldn't keep it up inside the woman, the zombie, the dirtwalker, not a *she* but an *it*, and when he looked down he saw he was fucking Lavender St. John, and he got hard again, and her rotten crusty saggy tits were full and round now, and he wanted to kiss them, but Lavender St. John's face split apart to show him something horrible underneath, and her nipples opened up and stared up at him, and he couldn't finish, and he screamed and jumped off the car, off the dirtwalker zombie chick woman thing *it*, and they all laughed and said it didn't matter that he couldn't finish, he was one of them now, and he really ought to pull up his pants so he didn't embarrass himself, and Deadbeat put one hand on the dirtwalker's cold leathery tit before putting a bullet in its brain, and Rotgut slapped Ace on the back and said, "Nice going."

And he said, "You plowed your first dirtwalker."

And he said, "You're a Necro Fiend now."

And he said, "*Swerdlow.*"

"I told you not to call me that, asshole. It's *Ace*," Ace said. He buckled his belt and scratched at his crotch, wondering if the dirtwalker's rotten loins could infect him.

"*Mira,* check out the big man," Rotgut said. "He plows his first dirtwalker, and now he's got a swollen head."

Was that a joke? Swollen head, like his dick was infected now? Like the green decay he could feel creeping through his balls was a joke because they drugged him up and made him plow a dirtwalker? They probably never even did it themselves. They were probably having a good laugh at him right now. *Look at the white boy fucking that zombie—can't wait to tell everyone at school what a freak Swerdlow really is.* The infection would probably kill him, and they would laugh and tell everyone he died because he was so pathetic he couldn't even lose it to a real girl, he had to fuck a dirtwalker, and when Ace's body got reanimated, they'd just use him for target practice like they didn't even know who he was, like he was never one of them, just some dumbass white boy, some stupid kid named—

"Swerdlow," Rotgut taunted.

"Fuck you!"

Ace shoved him, and Rotgut tripped backward, off balance. He slammed into a metal door in the cement wall, knocking it open and tumbling inside. He leapt out again a moment later, his face white with fear.

"Shit!"

Dirtwalkers were everywhere, pouring through the black doorway, their skeletal fingers groping the air for the fresh meat all around them.

The drug chose that moment to kick in again, blasting through Ace's brain one last time.

Things got gray around the edges.

There were blackouts.

Freeze-frames.

He noticed Saw Boy's chainsaw sitting on the floor by the red Chevy's busted right headlight, its motionless blade pointing into the air.

He heard gunshots and the sound of Thorazine Joe's baseball bat.

He heard screaming, but saw only dirtwalkers falling around him, with bullet holes in their foreheads or their skulls snapped off. Dirtwalkers didn't scream. Maybe it was him.

Strong, sharp fingers—brown bones held together by yellow cartilage and ragged strips of green-gray flesh, the color of institution walls, the color of the halls at P.S. 38—tried to grab his shoulder, but he knocked the hand away and Deadbeat put a bullet in the back of the dirtwalker's hairy, grinning skull. What was left of its right eye blasted out of the socket and landed on Ace's shirt. He flicked it off, terrified of touching it.

Mayhem. The air reeked of gun smoke, dry rot and the paprika tang of blood dust. Bodies littered the floor, their skull faces frozen in grinning rictus masks.

The chainsaw was still on the floor by the car.

Deadbeat tossed Ace a gun. It twisted in the air, its gleaming silver body folding in on itself and sprouting eyes and teeth and dozens of twitching, stick-like legs. He didn't remember catching it—why would he want to touch such a thing?—but suddenly it was a gun again and he was pulling the trigger and watching heads explode in shards of bone and chunks of dry flesh. The kickback was stronger than he'd expected. It threw him off balance.

Another blackout; like a blink, except everything was different when the lights came on again. Deadbeat, Rotgut and Thorazine Joe were standing back-to-back, knee-deep in dirtwalker bodies, and the guns were roaring and the bat was swinging and there were only a few zombies left.

One came at Rotgut, its face like a shrieking banshee, knotted strands of long gray hair trickling from its flaking scalp, the torn remains of a blue dress hanging off its bones. Rotgut lifted his silver six-shooter and aimed it at the zombie's head. The gun clicked loud and empty.

"Fuck!"

"Here!" Ace called, tossing his gun over. Rotgut snatched it out of the air, shoved it into the zombie's forehead, and blew it straight to Hell.

"Thanks, Ace," Rotgut said.

Ace. Not Swerdlow. Not dickwad. Ace.

Another blackout, shorter than before.

The chainsaw was still on the floor, and Saw Boy...

Saw Boy was standing a few feet away, just staring at him. His mouth moved like he was trying to say something. He was wearing a strange-colored scarf.

The Ace's vision cleared.

The dirtwalker standing behind Saw Boy was a real rotter, one of the worst Ace had ever seen. Its face was like melted rolls of flesh sagging on top of each other. Its gaping mouth was black with filth, and its eyes were barely visible between the drooping bags of discolored skin covering its bald head. The gnarled fingers of its hands were around Saw Boy's neck. Its overlong nails dug into the soft flesh of his throat and pulled it apart. Blood spilled from the gash, a waterfall of arterial spray, washing over the dirtwalker's fingers and down the front of Saw Boy's shirt.

Another blackout, and Ace was sitting in his boyhood kitchen watching his grandmother pull the skin off a roast chicken with her long, red nails.

Cool air touched his face. Ace was outside, walking home, back along Atlantic Avenue in the dark. Deadbeat and Rotgut were in front of him, and Thorazine Joe was limping at his side. He didn't see Saw Boy anywhere. His throat felt clogged with vomit, and his crotch felt raw.

No one spoke.

He didn't know what time it was, or how long it had been since the last blackout. The drug was sliding out of his system, clearing his mind. He felt heavier now. And dirty, unbelievably dirty, inside and out. He could stand under a hot shower, scrub himself with a loofah sponge until his skin was red and raw, and he still wouldn't feel clean. He thought he never would.

He felt sick. And something else. Something that tugged at his chest and made him empty inside. Something they all knew. Something that kept them quiet as they walked home. Even Rotgut, who never gave his jaw a rest.

Saw Boy was dead. His body lay back in the garage somewhere, his throat torn out, his shirt wet with blood. In a few hours, Saw Boy would rise again, stand up like it was nothing more than a good night's sleep, but he wouldn't be Saw Boy anymore. He'd be just another dirtwalker.

Ace's knees were weak. Walking was difficult. He didn't know if he was going to throw up or cry. He tried walking faster, but it only made him stumble, and that only made everything inside him more urgent. He had to get home. He couldn't wait to get home. He could cry and throw up and wash himself for as long as he wanted when he was home. Maybe his mother would be awake, sitting in the kitchen in her big cotton nightgown with hot chocolate ready. She would hug him and not ask any questions and tell him everything would be okay, that he wasn't bad, that he wasn't dirty, that he was safe now and he was only a kid and they would take care of him and protect him.

"Hey!" The voice, loud and sharp, startled them all. Ace nearly screamed and choked back a sob desperate to get out.

A policeman faced them from the street, sitting high on a brown and white horse. Ace was so lost in his own head he hadn't heard the horse approach. Deadbeat turned and raised his hand to make Thorazine Joe stop. Rotgut frowned and shuffled his feet.

"You kids okay?" the cop asked.

"Yeah," Deadbeat said.

"You know you're not supposed to be out this late. It's after curfew."

Ace tried to watch the cop's eyes, but he couldn't concentrate. The horse shifted its weight from one side to the other, then back again.

"I know," Deadbeat said. "My brother, he's retarded, and he wandered off after dinner." He squeezed Thorazine Joe's hand, a signal, and Joe started drooling and moaning. "We just found him now. We really have to get home. You won't lock us up, will you? He won't be able to take it if you lock us up."

The cop didn't say anything. Ace could feel his eyes looking each of them over. He wondered if the cop could see the blood dust staining their clothes in the dark. He wondered if the cop could see how dirty he felt.

"No," the policeman said. "You boys get on home now. Quick. It's Halloween, and there are a lot of troublemakers out tonight, not to mention the reanimates. Your brother wanders off after curfew again, you call the police, okay? That's what we're here for."

"Thanks, officer," Deadbeat said. He grabbed Thorazine Joe's arm and tugged him away. Rotgut smiled and waved at the cop.

That was it. They were free to go. The three others continued down Atlantic Avenue toward Nevins Street, toward home, but Ace's legs didn't move. He stood where he was and couldn't take his eyes off the policeman.

Couldn't he see the filth inside Ace? Couldn't he see the rot?

"Something the matter?" the cop asked.

The thing pulling at Ace's chest expanded, reaching out for the policeman, yearning for something Ace couldn't put a word to.

The others stopped and turned around. "Hey, come on," Deadbeat called.

Ace's mouth opened, but nothing came out. His whole body

felt tense, explosive. Something had to give.

"You all right?" the cop said.

"Let's get going already," Deadbeat said.

In his mind, Ace saw the female zombie squirming under him on the hood of the car. He could still feel its papery, chafing flesh against him, all over him. He could see the others holding it down, Saw Boy right next to him, gripping one of its thrashing legs. He felt the itch in his crotch where he'd touched the thing's rotten flesh, and he wondered if he was going to die.

"Is there something you want to tell me, son?" the cop said.

He could still see the zombie shredding the flesh of Saw Boy's neck, and the blood, Christ, all the blood. Saw Boy was dead, and he'd put his thing inside a dirtwalker—who was she when she was alive? Someone's sister? Wife? Mother?—and they were all going to Hell for it. They were all rotting inside.

"Come on, Ace," Rotgut called.

Ace looked up at the cop and opened his mouth. "I—"

It was all he could get out before his chin started quivering. The floodgates were dangerously close to opening, and if they opened Ace knew there'd be no stopping it.

What if he said something, told the cop what happened? Ace could picture the consequences: jail, humiliation, his parents' anger and disappointment; but more than that, he could see Big Louis pounding him in the schoolyard, kids writing *white boy* on his locker again, laughing at him in gym class when he missed a shot, whispering *bitch* at him when they passed in the halls. Worst of all, Shaniqua would ignore him like she used to. She would never smile at him again.

He'd come too far for that, been through too much. It was time for respect to be paid. Even Rotgut wasn't calling him *Swerdlow* anymore. He had street cred now.

Everything else, all the target practice and plowing and death, the whole horror show, was a small price to pay.

The cop leaned forward in his saddle.

"Tomorrow's a school day," Ace said, and ran to catch up with the others.

THE BEAT OF HER WINGS

Here's another example of a story that took a while to find its true self. I first wrote "The Beat of Her Wings," in its entirety, in a half-hour session of furious keyboard pounding. As you might imagine for something that was banged out in thirty minutes, it was terrible. It was also very different from what you see here. For one thing, it was a humor piece. For another, it was written as a monologue, Margaret talking to Max in her head as she's driving home. Sometimes you've just got to put stories away for a while before you can get a handle on them, and that's what I did with "The Beat of Her Wings." So here it is, making a public appearance for the first time in its much-improved form.

She steps on the accelerator, pushing the speedometer's needle up past eighty, and grips the steering wheel so hard she imagines her knuckles breaking through the skin. Pale tree trunks loom out of the dark and whip by in the headlights. All around her, a web of old, abandoned roads cuts through the dusty flatland, shrouded in night.

Her breath comes shallowly. She can't stop trembling. One sweaty palm slips from the steering wheel, and the car nearly veers off the road. She rights it, curses, and checks the rearview mirror. She checks the sky.

The night is too dark to see anything. There's no sound other than the rev of her engine. She wonders if her pursuer has given up. No, there, she sees it, a dark silhouette crossing the moon. And now she hears it again, the unmistakable sound of wings thundering in the night, creating a strong downdraft that shakes the car.

The sound matches the drumbeat thudding in her head: *Max...Max...Max...*

The start of it all.

The first time Margaret lied to Max—*really* lied, not the little white lies a wife tells her husband on occasion—it was harder than she thought it would be. She sat at the breakfast table and played nervously with her teacup, wondering if a lie was okay if it was for the right reasons. Across from her, Max ate the eggs she fried for him like clockwork every morning and flipped through an issue of *National Geographic*, occasionally chuckling and shaking his head over some discovery he was sure they'd gotten wrong. As he'd often reminded her throughout their seventeen years of marriage, he was the only paleontologist these days who knew shit from shinola.

The passing years hadn't marred his looks. He was still a beautiful creature, with a strong jawline, thick hair, and sharp clear eyes that could make you feel like you were the only one in the room who mattered. The gray that salted his temples made him even more handsome, she thought. She used to love him so much. She couldn't remember why anymore, only that there'd been a time when they'd burned for each other. A time when she never had to lie.

"Busy one today," she said, and he looked up from the magazine. "I'm going to be out all day. I have a ton of errands to run before dinner." It was a quick fabrication off the top of her head. She'd heard somewhere that it was best to keep lies simple.

And yet she couldn't look him in the eye, and her hands shook so violently they set her teacup chittering against its saucer. She stuffed her hands in her lap. Her face felt hot. She thought for sure Max would know she was lying, but instead he nodded and said, "I'm out all day, too, Margie." His nickname for her. The name of a child. She hated it. "I've got a faculty meeting at AU that'll probably go to four or five."

She knew there was no faculty meeting at the school today, and hearing how easily the lie slipped from his mouth put an ache in her chest. He didn't bat an eyelash. His face stayed as pale and cool as alabaster. Max knew how to lie. He had experience.

Her hands stopped shaking and balled themselves into fists.

She made sure he saw her leave the house and get into her car. Rolling down the long dirt driveway that led from their house in the woods to Outlander Road below, she wondered how long it would take Max to make the phone call. Would make a mad dash for the handset the moment he heard her car start, or would he count to a hundred to be certain she was gone first?

She turned onto Outlander and drove until the road forked. To her left was the highway that led to the city of Alvarez and beyond it to Cheyenne, the state capitol. To her right, a single sawhorse blocked the entrance to the old mining roads that branched all the way out to the canyons. They'd been abandoned years ago, but had so far remained ungentrified by the Starbucks, pizza joints, and housing developments that were spreading out from the city like a wildfire as the Alvarez University of Arts and Sciences—AU, as Max called it—gained prestige. It was still just miles of trees and empty, unpaved road, and that made it the perfect place to hide the car.

She walked back home through the woods until she saw the upstairs windows of their house peeking through the net of tree branches. A modest bi-level, it was all they could afford on Max's university salary. Built in the Thirties, it still had the original wainscoting and thick, wood-paneled doors with old-fashioned keyholes, though the keys themselves, which she imagined to be brass and cartoonishly large like the keys in old movies, were long lost. The old wood creaked and groaned at night like a dying animal, though sometimes she thought she was the only one who heard it. Max had fallen in love with the house right away, especially after the cramped quarters they'd endured in New York back when he worked at the American Museum of Natural History, but to her a house sitting alone in the middle of a forest felt like a prison. Their nearest neighbors were a mile down Outlander. Margaret didn't even know their names.

She went around to the back of the house, ducking past the windows in case Max was watching, and entered through the cellar door. She hid in the dark down there, cobwebs sticking to her hair, the old water heater ticking like a time bomb beside her, and wondered if all forty-six-year-old housewives sneaked into their own homes and hid in the basement. Maybe this was her own special punishment.

She held her breath when she heard a car pull up to the house. When the doorbell rang, her heart jumped into her throat, and she listened to Max's footsteps clomping above her head. The click of the doorknob, the squeak of hinges, and then a female voice, high and chirpy, so coy it made her skin crawl.

"Good morning, Professor."

A girlish giggle, followed by the low rumble of Max's voice. More footsteps. She followed their steps and realized he was taking her into his study. Something tart rose at the back of Margaret's throat. She swallowed it down.

She didn't really want to see, but she knew she had to. It was the only way to be certain. Steeling herself, she crept up the stairs that led to the kitchen. She took off her shoes and padded quietly to the door of Max's study, then squatted to peek through the old keyhole.

Max was inside, and so was a brown-haired girl Margaret recognized from his paleontology class. Susie-something? The girl's name escaped her, but she looked like a Susie anyway, lean and smooth-skinned and giggling while Max nuzzled her neck. She was leaning back against his desk. The strap of her camisole had fallen, her long hair fanning out over her bare shoulder. Max's slacks were hung over the desk chair. The same slacks Margaret had stayed up late ironing for him.

The girl, Susie-something, looked about twenty. Half Margaret's age. No, less than half, she corrected herself. The ache in her chest intensified. But worse than the hurt was the shame that came with knowing she'd willfully ignored the signs that had been there all along. Max had stopped showing any interest in her years ago, even before they moved to Wyoming. Only now did she understand the extent to which she'd lied to herself, convinced herself every day that Max was too tired from work to touch her. She'd even blamed herself for a while, worrying about her weight and what gravity was doing to her now that she was closer to fifty than forty. She'd joined a gym in town and taken rock-climbing classes, thinking maybe if she toned up she'd catch his eye again. But with the young, pretty students he took on every semester, and all those nights he didn't come home until she was already asleep, the clues kept mounting, nagging at her until she was forced to hide in her own home and spy through a keyhole like a Peeping Tom.

She wished she were far away. She wished wings would sprout from her back so she could leap into the sky and take flight, flap them so hard it would blow the whole house to splinters.

Claws scratch at the roof of the car. The sound is like nails on a chalkboard, only harder, more insistent, as the claws scrabble for a hold and try to tear through the car's metal skin. The noise sets her teeth on edge. She leans on the accelerator. The engine revs, roars, and the dirt road unspools toward her in the headlights.

She turns the wheel, zig-zags in tight swerves. In the rearview mirror, she sees her pursuer fall behind again, lost in the clouds of dust thrown up in her wake. She takes a deep breath and relaxes her iron grip on the wheel. Her hands shake so much her wedding ring taps against the steering wheel. It sounds almost like a child's toy drum.

Margaret bought a new dress for the cocktail party at the university president's house. A slinky black sleeveless number, it was tight enough to show off the body she'd earned at the gym and low cut enough to reveal more cleavage than she normally would. Max hardly noticed, even when she shrugged sinuously out of her coat as they arrived. Maybe the dress had been a mistake. And her haircut, she felt anxious about that, too. She'd had her roots touched up and her locks chopped into a smart, shiny bob. The hairstyle of a twenty-something. Who was she kidding?

She stepped into the enormous living room, where the furniture had been moved to make room for a bar by the wall and a central table of hors d'oeuvres. Max's colleagues from the science department mingled with the crowd, all tweed and spectacles and tightly trimmed beards. The party was being held in their honor, celebrating a major grant from a research corporation, and they strutted from handshake to handshake like cocks of the block.

Max headed for the bar, leaving her wondering what to do with herself. He *had* to have noticed the dress, she thought. She turned, hoping to see him sneaking a glance back at her, but all she saw was the back of his head as he worked his way through the crowd around the bar.

Fine. She popped a piece of shrimp from the hors d'oeuvres table into her mouth. Around her, student caterers in rented tuxedoes circulated with silver trays, collecting napkins and empty glasses from the guests. She wondered if little Susie-something was among them, if she would have the nerve to show up knowing Margaret would be there. She didn't know what she'd do if she saw the girl. Throw a drink in her face? Punch her in the nose? Or would she smile sweetly and shake the little slut's hand like she didn't suspect a thing, like she hadn't been keeping this terrible knowledge locked inside her for a week since spying on the two of them in Max's study?

A high-pitched squeal drew her attention to a group of people nearby. A curly-haired woman stood laughing with her friends, gently rocking a stroller in front of her. Inside, a baby wrapped in a tiny blue blanket squealed again and pulled at the matching blue bonnet on his head.

Margaret turned away, suddenly dizzy. She could smell again the antiseptic odor of ammonia and pink hand soap that had permeated the clinic in New York, and Max's voice on the phone, *Is it done yet? I'm sorry, but you know I don't want children. I told you that from the start.*

She'd made sacrifices for the sake of their marriage. She'd left behind a career because Max didn't want her to work; left New York behind because Max had a job opportunity in Alvarez. And then there was what she'd left behind at the clinic.

What had Max given up for her?

"Margaret," someone called. She looked up, thinking it might be Max. Instead, when the crowd parted, she saw it was Bentley Kirkland, vice-president of acquisitions at the Cheyenne Museum of Science. The museum had close ties with the university, though for whatever reason Bentley and Max refused to work together. What began as a professional rivalry between them had turned into genuine animosity. She thought it was ridiculous, like two little boys fighting over who had the most toys.

Bentley moved through the crowd toward her the way a gator moved through swamp water, sinuous and single-minded. "You look amazing," he said. He kissed her cheek and lingered a moment. "Did you do something to your hair?" Ever the ladies' man.

Bentley was handsome, tall and angular, with the confidence of a man who knew how to get what he wanted. Margaret found him arrogant and smug. She didn't like the way he showed up at these events with a different woman on his arm each time, or the way he flirted so openly with her on the rare occasions when he came alone. And though it was embarrassing to admit, his prosthetic leg disturbed her. She'd seen it once when she spotted him in shorts on the elliptical at the gym. She'd stared at it a moment before ducking unnoticed into her rock-climbing class. Something about its shiny pink color and shaft-like rigidity alarmed her.

"Hello, Bentley," she said, forcing a smile.

"Nice to see you out among the living," he said. With his black hair slicked back and his aquiline nose, she thought he looked like an exotic bird of prey. "Honestly, I don't know why Max keeps you cooped up in that house in the middle of Timbuktu. A woman like you ought to be paraded around town and shown off to jealous friends, not locked away like Rapunzel. Especially not in that dress." She could feel his eyes roving all over her body. It sickened her, and yet...

And yet, at least someone was paying attention to her. Noticing her.

"Max likes his privacy," she told him. She looked toward the bar and saw Max was still with the bartender, a tuxedoed girl with a long blonde ponytail. Another student caterer, she barely looked old enough to drink, let alone tend bar. Max leaned in close to the girl, said something, and they both laughed. Ice filled Margaret's belly, and she quickly turned away.

Bentley lifted his glass to his lips and muttered, "His privacy? Yes, I'm sure he does."

Margaret stared at her shoes, only half listening. "Don't we all?" she asked.

He finished his drink and licked his lips. "You know, there's something quite nice about having friends in high places. For instance, I have this friend at the American Museum of Natural History in New York who loves to gossip. She tells me all sorts of interesting things."

She looked up at him. "That's where Max used to work."

"Indeed. In fact, one of her more amusing stories is about him. But surely you already know it, the story of why our dear Max had to leave the museum and drag you out west?" Margaret didn't answer. "Ashley Winstone. You've heard that name, of course?" Margaret looked down at the shrimp bowl. She wished Bentley would go away. She didn't want to hear any of it. "No, I suppose you wouldn't have. Max certainly wouldn't tell you, and the museum kept it all very hush-hush to protect their reputation. The girl lost her college internship, since their relationship was hardly professional, and Max, well, after the museum fired him, an offer from a university out in Wyoming must have suddenly looked very tempting. So now he's here, among all these young, impressionable students who look up to him, while he keeps you locked away in a house in the woods."

Shut up, she thought. Shut up shut up shut up.

"Interesting story, don't you think?" He took another sip from his glass. The corners of his mouth curled into a shark's smile.

She stormed to the bar. Max was still joking with the girl, holding a wineglass for Margaret in one hand and his own half-finished scotch in the other.

"I want to go," Margaret blurted, interrupting them. She glared at the girl, who frowned and wandered off to serve another guest.

"Now?" Max said. "We just got here."

"Yes, now."

He looked at her like he was drowning and she was the rock tied to his ankle. "Come on, Margie, we can't. I have to at least say hello to the president and press some flesh. This is a big day for us."

"How much longer?" she demanded.

He shrugged and handed over her wineglass. "I don't know, twenty minutes, half an hour."

She sat down on a divan near the door. "Fine," she said. "I'll wait here. If you're not back in twenty minutes, I'm taking the car and you can call a cab."

He sighed. "What's gotten into you?"

"Nothing lately."

His jaw tightened. "What's that supposed to mean?"

"Whatever you want it to mean. Go press your flesh or whatever it is you need to do."

"Jesus," Max muttered, and disappeared into the crowd. Margaret sank back against the wall, downed her wine in a single gulp, and checked her watch. She wished she were invisible.

Susie-something wasn't Max's first infidelity. She'd suspected as much, but to *know*, to be told so bluntly, so callously, put a knot of barbed wire in her chest. Worse, it seemed like everyone else knew before she did. Probably, it was the talk of the party. She pictured the guests dipping their shrimp in cocktail sauce and whispering, *That poor woman. Still, she should've known. Ugly old cow like that, how could she possibly compete?*

She eyed the door. Why was she staying? The car was right outside. She could drive and drive and not stop she was miles away from Max and all the mounting humiliations. She imagined wings sprouting from her back again. Fly away, little bird.

Bentley emerged from the crowd, heading for the door to make an early exit. Lucky him, she thought. He buttoned his smart blazer as he approached, and she noticed how broad it made his shoulders look. She caught herself staring and stood up to move away from him, but then, suddenly, he was right in front of her. He took her hand, said, "If you ever want to talk," and pressed his business card into her palm.

Faster, faster, she thinks, pedal to the metal. The beat of enormous wings is so close by it's like a heartbeat in the night. The roof of the car puckers down toward her. A talon breaks through the metal, white bone with rusty streaks of drying blood. She tries not to think about whose blood it is.

She pulls the steering wheel to one side, then the other, trying to shake off her pursuer. The talon slips out, and a shrill cry pierces the night. But she knows her pursuer is too stubborn to give up the chase. Already she feels wind from the wings battering her car, practically blowing her off the road.

Something in the road, a pothole or a dead animal, bumps under one wheel and jostles the car. She loses control of the vehicle. Her breath freezes in her chest. Time slows and speeds up simultaneously, warping like old wood. The wheels skid and scream. She smells burning rubber.

Struggling to right the car, she hears claws scratching at the roof again. She feels like screaming, feels like pulling madly at her hair. None of this can be happening. It can't be.

She meant to throw out Bentley's business card right away, but instead it lingered in her purse. She thought about the card as she sat at the kitchen table with Max's coffee and eggs cooling in front of his empty chair. Her so-called husband had come home late again last night. Margaret had pretended to be asleep when he finally slipped into their bed around three.

She opened the newspaper to take her mind off where he might have been. On the front page was a grainy photo of a half-demolished house on the outskirts of town. The roof was completely destroyed, leaving the structure looking like an opened cookie jar. The authorities were still trying to piece together what happened. Some thought it was a gas explosion, others said it was a freak weather occurrence. All anyone knew for sure was that the occupant of the house was missing.

Max barged into the kitchen then, his hair uncombed, his shirt half buttoned, with his tie draped around his collar. "Shit," he said. He grabbed his coffee and drank it quickly. He looked so greedy to her, gulping it down like that. Not caring about anything, just taking what he wanted. "I'm late. Why did you let me sleep?"

Margaret shrugged. "You looked like you needed the rest. Must have been a strenuous night."

Max ignored her remark and sat down, buttoning his shirt. "These midterms are killing me. I'll be grading at the school all night again. I'm sorry about that." Just before he buttoned his collar, she noticed a bright red smear on his neck. Lipstick. Susie-something, or the blonde bartender from the party? Or a new one she didn't know about?

Margaret took his plate off the table and scraped the eggs into the trash.

"What the hell?" Max gaped at her, holding his fork over the empty spot where his plate had been, a pathetic devil with a tiny pitchfork.

She wanted to tell him she knew everything, that leaving lipstick on his neck for her to see was like an extra slap in the face, but the idea of bringing everything out into the open terrified her, so instead she said, "You're late. You should go."

His face flushed with anger. "Christ, Margie, you've been impossible for days now, ever since the party. What the hell is wrong with you?"

"My name isn't Margie," she said as she walked out of the kitchen. "It's Margaret."

After Max left for work, she fished the card from her purse, called Bentley, and drove to Cheyenne. When she walked into Bentley's basement office at the museum, neither of them said much. They both knew why she was there. He locked the door and pulled a box of condoms from his desk—unopened, still in the bag from the drug store, as if he'd been expecting her—and he gave a smug, triumphant smile. They had sex on his big leather office couch under a framed print of a Tyrannosaurus rex skeleton half-embedded in stone. They didn't kiss or look each other in the eye. She thought of Max the whole time, how wonderfully hurt he'd be when he found out, and that made it easier to let this man she hated touch her.

Afterward, lying with their bare skin sticking to the leather, she couldn't stop staring at his prosthetic leg. There was a chip in the knee she hadn't noticed before, shaped roughly like the state of New Jersey. Was it new, she wondered, or was it just that she'd never been this close before?

Bentley caught her staring and said, "I lost it to gangrene during an expedition in Burma about fifteen years ago."

Margaret pulled her gaze away from the plastic limb. "Is that true?"

He gave her a look that said, "Does it matter?" and got up and walked toward the private bathroom on the other side of his office. "I've got a busy afternoon. You should probably get going," he said. Then he added, "Don't forget your earrings," and his tone of voice told her women had left things behind before, maybe married women like her, and it had gotten him in trouble. Not enough to change his ways, oh no, not Bentley Kirkland, playboy of the paleontology set, but enough to teach him not to leave any further evidence of indiscretions.

The bathroom door clicked shut, and Margaret regarded her clothes piled messily on the carpet. Had she really just cheated on her husband? She expected to feel empowered after giving Max a taste of his own medicine, but instead she felt sick at how easily and irreversibly she'd sunk to Max's level. She dressed quickly, wanting to get away as fast as she could. Grabbing her earrings off the desk, she noticed a long piece of paper spread over the blotter, held in place with paperweights. It was a map, the terrain represented by jagged twisty lines like a child's drawing of a tree, a red circle drawn around one branch. Something about it looked familiar to her, but she couldn't place where she'd seen it before. The toilet flushed then, and Bentley came out, looking surprised that she was still there.

She tapped the map. "Where is this?"

Bentley sat on the couch to pull his underwear and pants over his prosthetic leg. "Red Creek Canyon."

Ah, no wonder it had looked familiar. Not long ago, her rock-climbing class had taken a field trip there. The Parks Department had given them maps just like Bentley's and warned them that most of canyon was too dangerous for hiking or climbing. Every year people disregarded the warnings and disappeared, they said, presumably falling into deep crevices or getting buried under rockslides. All manner of ignoble death seemed to wait just past the locked gates and fences, so Margaret's class had climbed the easier rock faces and rewarded themselves with a picnic at the top of the canyon. She'd spotted an old gate there labeled 4 WEST, blocking access to the off-limits areas. The padlock was broken. She'd been tempted to sneak a peek beyond, but then her instructor had called her back.

"Are you going hiking?" she asked Bentley, then remembered his leg and winced.

He stood and continued dressing. "No, someone called the museum, one of those extreme sports maniacs. He said he went climbing in one of the restricted gorges and discovered a cave in a cliff filled with dinosaur eggs. Perfectly preserved specimens. Apparently he took one with him as proof, but when I called him back, it went straight to voicemail. I've been trying ever since, but no luck. It's too bad. There are so few new finds these days. The museum would have paid him quite a bit. I'm guessing he got a better offer from somewhere else, maybe New York. It's become a very competitive field." He shrugged. "Still, the possibilities are fascinating. Triceratops, Tyrannosaurus rex, Corythosaurus, all manner of pterosaurs; dinosaurs were all over this part of the country during the Cretaceous Period, but no one has ever found completely intact eggs until now. Have you heard of the Chalumna Principle?"

She shook her head. "Max never mentioned it."

"Of course not. He doesn't believe in it. I do. I've been writing about it in the journals for years." Bentley was showing off for her, she realized. He wanted her to see how smart he was, smarter than Max. He grew more animated as he spoke, and Margaret couldn't help noticing he seemed more alive and passionate now than when he'd been screwing her. "The Chalumna River in South Africa is where Captain Goosen caught a Coelacanth fish in 1938. What's remarkable about that particular fish is that everyone thought it had gone extinct sixty million years earlier. Instead, a delicate balance of temperature and isolation factors had allowed the Coelacanth not only to survive but to do so unnoticed for millennia. The Chalumna Principle basically states that unique attributes of certain locations—temperature, isolation, food supplies—can defy every cornerstone of the natural sciences, from decomposition rates to fossilization to extinction itself. It's not a very popular idea, but despite the opinions of stubborn idiots like Max, it's real enough. If those eggs are as perfectly preserved as they've been described, it could help prove the theory. At this point, I'm thinking of putting together my own team and retrieving them myself." He tapped the red circle on the map. "Right here, in this cave, is a scientific discovery too big to ignore. So I'm sure you'll understand that I need to get back to work now."

And there it was, the brush-off, as clear as day. He didn't kiss her when she left, not even on the cheek. He just muttered goodbye and reached for the phone. On the drive home, Margaret burst into tears. Seeing Bentley had been a mistake. He didn't care about her. She'd known that from the start, of course. He only wanted her because of his childish rivalry with Max, but some part of her had hoped she would at least matter to him. To anyone. Instead, she'd only proved herself to be irrelevant once again.

Enough, she thought, wiping away her tears. She wanted out. She wanted a chance to start over. But more than anything, she wanted to prove to both Max and Bentley that she wasn't a fool who could be taken for granted.

By the time she reached home, a plan was already taking shape in her mind. It was Bentley who'd inadvertently handed her the perfect way to show them both up at the same time, and in the process acquire enough money to move out and hire a good divorce lawyer. A nest egg—wasn't that what they called it? How ironic.

How big were dinosaur eggs anyway? They couldn't be too big if the man who'd called Bentley had taken one home. Depending on how many there were, she could take them all and hide them from Max in the trunk of her car until she sold them to the museum. She'd sell them directly to Bentley so she could watch his smug smile fade when he realized she'd beaten him to it, that she'd scooped him and Max both with the find of a lifetime.

But would she even recognize a dinosaur egg if she saw it?

It would be fossilized, which meant it probably looked like a rock to the untrained eye. It would be easy to miss. If she was going to do this, she needed to know what she was looking for. She made a beeline for Max's study, where he kept his science journals and reference guides locked behind the glass doors of the bookcases. She searched for the key among the tall piles of papers and folders on his desk, praying it wasn't on the ring in his pocket. Eventually, she found it in the top drawer. She reached for the key, then froze. Beside it was an open, half empty box of condoms. Max kept them in his desk just like Bentley did. The two of them were more alike than they knew.

She considered throwing the box in the trashcan under the desk so he'd find it and know she'd discovered his secret. Instead she left it in the drawer. The look on his face when she claimed the eggs would be ten times more satisfying. A hundred times.

The front door slammed, startling her, and she heard Max's footsteps in the hallway. He was home early. She panicked a moment, wondering if he'd brought one of his floozies home with him. She slid the drawer closed just as Max appeared in the doorway. To her relief, he was alone.

"What are you doing in here?" he asked. He sounded both nervous and angry. His eyes kept darting toward the desk.

"Just tidying up," she said, surprised at how calm she sounded. "Someone has to. It's a mess in here."

His face hardened. "I don't want you in here. I don't want you going through my things."

"Max, I just—"

"Everything is exactly where it's supposed to be, where I can find it. I don't want you touching anything."

She held up her hands. "All right. Jesus. I didn't mean any harm."

"I don't care, just stay out of this room." He grabbed the doorknob and said, "Let's go."

She walked past him out of the study, and as Max closed the door she wondered if he could smell Bentley's scent on her. She hoped so. She hoped it burned his nostrils like bleach.

The speedometer needle hovers just below 90, and the sound

of wings grows distant. She hears her pursuer flapping harder, trying to keep up. Just as she thinks she might have a chance, might actually get away, the engine starts to cough and groan. Steam billows out from under the hood. It's only a matter of time before the car will stall on her. She screams, and bangs her fists against the steering wheel.

Stay focused, some calm part of her says. You're almost home, and then everything will be fine.

—How will everything be fine? What do I do then?

—Isn't it obvious?

It is, of course. It's so obvious she can't help grinning. She leans on the accelerator, her own laughter ringing in her ears.

Margaret woke just past midnight from a dream in which she came home to find Max and Susie-something laughing at her from her own bed. After a week of sneaking into Max's study to read up, and another week of trying to muster the courage to put her plan into action, she took the dream as a sign that it was time. She left the bed quietly, pulled her rock-climbing gear from the closet, and glanced at Max sleeping peacefully on his side of the bed. He'd sneaked in late again. She wondered which of the girls had exhausted him this time, then decided it didn't matter anymore. In his post-coital state, he'd sleep straight through until morning. He wouldn't even know she was gone.

It took an hour to drive the deserted mining roads off Outlander to Red Creek Canyon, and another twenty minutes along the narrow road on the other side of the broken 4 WEST gate before she reached the section that had been marked on Bentley's map. Setting up the rope anchor at the edge of the cliff, she looked down into the darkness and felt dizzy knowing it masked a drop of hundreds of feet to the jagged stones that lined the river below. The light from her headlamp barely penetrated the inky blackness.

Margaret tightened the harness around her, took a deep breath, and rappelled down. Her arms shook and her fingers felt sore, but she reminded herself she'd done this before in class and could do it again now. She didn't descend very far before her headlamp revealed a cave etched into the cliff like a gaping maw. She swung inside and disconnected herself from the rope. Before her, a tall, wide cavern extended deep into the cliffside, everything quickly fading to black outside the range of her light. The air in the cave was warmer, humid, and something smelled awful. The sharp *plink* of dripping water echoed somewhere deep within the darkness. The cave floor rose on a slight incline before her, carpeted with slippery moss. She took a few careful steps until something hard crunched under her. Looking down, she saw a long white object that bent in an arc beneath her shoe. A bone. The rib of an animal.

Her headlamp revealed more bones scattered across the cave floor: the antlered skulls of deer, the elongated scapulas of coyotes. There must be another entrance to the cave deep in the hills, she thought. The animals had gotten in but couldn't find their way out again, lost in the dark. And yet there were so many bones.

Just ahead she saw a shallow, bowl-shaped dip in the floor, and within it, dozens of ovoid stones. No, not stones, she realized; eggs, each slightly larger than a softball, brown like rock but with a pocked, leathery surface. She'd expected to find them buried in sediment, had even brought tools to chip them free, but these eggs looked so perfect, so ready to be plucked from their resting place that the sight of them took her breath away. For a moment, she understood Max's love for his work. The same rush he must have felt on his first dig sparked through her now, and suddenly she wasn't angry anymore. She wanted to share it with him, bring him back an egg and make him love her again, make everything go back to the way it was when they still burned for each other.

But it was too late for that. There had been too many betrayals. She needed to stick to the plan, put the eggs in the trunk and take control of her life.

Approaching the eggs, her foot hit something that skittered across the ground. It was long, skinny, and coiled, and she jumped back, thinking it was a snake. When it didn't move again she realized it was only a nylon rope, braided blue and yellow. A climbing rope, like hers. One end was frayed, as if it had been yanked forcefully out of its anchor. The other end snaked to a small mound of equipment she hadn't noticed before: harnesses, a cracked helmet with its light missing, bent carabiners, all resting on what she thought was a pile of twigs. But then she saw the round, terminal knob of a femur poking out of the pile, and realized they weren't twigs at all. They were bones, broken, shattered, and dripping with something thick and slimy.

At the top of the mound was a shiny pink prosthetic leg. On its knee, a New Jersey-shaped chip.

Bentley. He'd come with a team from the museum to stake his claim, but something had gotten them first. Something in the cave.

The animal bones, that awful carrion smell...

How soon would it be back? Or was it still here?

She turned back to the eggs. Her instincts screamed at her to run, but she refused to leave without what she'd come for. She reached for an egg and lifted it easily off the ground, but her nervous hands trembled and she dropped it. It landed on the floor just outside the bowl, and the sharp *clack* of its shell echoed loudly through the cave.

Something shifted in the dark behind the nest. Two eyes opened, as big as dinner plates, and reflected the light from her headlamp like mirrors. A loud screech threatened to burst her eardrums, and she put her hands over her ears.

It crawled out of the blackness on all fours, its hind legs scaly and taloned, its front legs not legs at all but folded wings, their pointed tips moving like leathery masts beside its spine. Even stooped over, the bird-like creature spanned more than a dozen feet from the ground to the bony crest that protruded from the back of its head. Something dangled from its long, toothless beak. Margaret couldn't tell what it was until she caught the glint of a wristwatch at one end, and then her stomach flipped over.

Bentley had been wrong about the eggs being fossils, but he'd been right about one thing. There were places in the world, pockets of frozen time, where life continued untouched by the iron law of extinction.

The creature, the pterosaur, the mama bird that should

have died off with the rest of her kind a hundred million years ago, tossed back her head so that the severed arm in her beak disappeared down her gullet. Then she took another step forward. Margaret backed away. The egg she'd dropped started to roll toward her down the incline of the cave floor. Margaret stopped it with her foot.

The pterosaur paused. Margaret lifted the egg. The pterosaur took a step back.

The creature was afraid of her, she realized with awe. Like any mama bird, the pterosaur was afraid Margaret was going to hurt her egg. She was waiting to see what Margaret would do next. As long as Margaret held the egg, she was safe. It was a stalemate.

Margaret backed toward the cave mouth, where her rope was waiting to take her back to the top of the canyon. The pterosaur inched forward, a shrill growl emanating from her throat. A warning that Margaret was pushing her luck. Margaret paused at the entrance, the cool night breeze from the canyon blowing at her back.

A voice floated out of the darkness, little more than a whisper, and it sent shivers down her back. "Margaret…" In the light of her headlamp, a bloody hand appeared from behind a heap of bones, and then she saw Bentley pull himself along the cave floor, his face slick with grue and dirt. "Margaret…," he groaned. She was too terrified to move. "For the love of God…" His hand stretched toward her.

The pterosaur dove for him, her beak snapping around him and lifting him into the air. Margaret screamed and grabbed the rope. She wrapped her thighs tight around it, and pulled herself upward with one arm while holding the egg to her side with the other. Bentley's screams followed her. When she reached the top of the canyon, a loud snap echoed out of the cave, and the screaming stopped.

In its place came an angry screech and the sound of wings unfurling.

Margaret ran for the car, flung open the door, and threw herself inside. Nestling the egg in her lap, she twisted the ignition key and stomped on the accelerator. The car sped forward, kicking up clouds of dirt. From behind her came the loud beat of wings as the pterosaur took off into the air.

She slows the car as she leaves the old mining roads and turns onto Outlander. She wants to give her pursuer a chance to catch up. After flying for over an hour, mama bird is tired. Only when Margaret hears scratching on the roof again does she step on the gas. The engine rattles and clangs. More steam pours from under the hood. She just needs the car to hold together a little longer.

In the rearview, by the dim pink light of the approaching dawn, she sees the pterosaur still following, working her exhausted wings. She's a fighter like me, Margaret thinks, she refuses to just roll over and accept what life throws her way. Margaret strokes the egg in her lap. She almost feels sorry for taking it and putting mama bird through this. She likes to think she would have been just as protective and determined a mother herself.

Bentley told her about the rock-climber who took an egg from the cave and then disappeared. It's obvious what happened. She saw the evidence in the newspaper, the photo of the demolished house, its roof torn away. There's no doubt in her mind that the pterosaur will go wherever her eggs go, and will attack anyone to get them back.

As Margaret turns onto the driveway leading to their lonely little house in the woods, she knows she'll never be able to sell the egg. Mama bird won't leave without it. But that's okay, because once she's home, everything will be fine.

Max, Max, Max, goes the drumbeat in her head, and each beat stabs with a serrated memory: Max and Susie-something behind the study door, Max flirting with the bartender, Max with lipstick on his neck. Margaret quietly sobbing with her feet in stirrups at the clinic. *Is it done yet?*

Her pursuer has fallen behind again. Margaret will have just enough time to leave the egg on the bed beside Max's sleeping form, then make her way down to the safety of the cellar.

The pterosaur will tear through everything—the roof, the bedroom, Max—to get her egg back. The damage to the house will be irreparable, but that's okay. Margaret can't live there anymore, not with all the bad memories. Her inheritance will buy her a new house. A new life. One where she might actually matter.

But for now, she will wait in the darkness of the cellar one last time, with her old friends the cobwebs and the water heater.

She will stand by the high, narrow windows that look out onto the dawn of a new day.

And she will listen for the beat of her wings.

TOAD LILY

*This next story is an experiment in implication. Everything impor-
tant is implied instead of shown, from the backstory to the climax to
the contents of that compost bin. I don't know if the experiment suc-
ceeded—it's not up to me to make that call—but I do like the clean
simplicity of this story. And all those definitions.*

Once, she thought she saw him on the Coney Island board-
walk, her little Billy-Toad, as the man she knew he would
have grown up to be: tall and lean, thick hair blowing in the
wind, his shoulders broad and strong. She hurried over to him,
waving her arms, calling his name, but when he turned around,
she saw he was actually an old Korean woman in a high-col-
lared floral silk dress.

She saw him other times, too. On the 86th Street cross-
town bus in Manhattan, she spotted him from the corner of her
eye, but when she turned, he revealed himself to be a young
schoolgirl reading a chemistry textbook. On Montague Street
in Brooklyn, during one of her therapeutic shopping sprees, she
saw him again, standing by the curb, but he was just a lamppost,
decorated with fliers for stoop sales and moving companies.

Each time Joyce saw him, each time she discovered it *wasn't*
him, it all came back to her: grief, pain, loss, confusion.

"You're losing it," Carl said. They ate lunch on the deck of their
Boerum Hill brownstone, overlooking the neglected garden in
their backyard. "Billy's gone. It's been a long time. We have to
try to pick up the pieces."

"I could've sworn it was him," she said. She poked at her uneaten sandwich, not wanting to look her husband in the eye.

He reached across the table to touch her hand, but she pulled back. His skin looked bloated, discolored, like Billy's did when she saw her boy through the glass in the little room under the hospital.

"You need something to occupy your mind," Carl said. "Maybe you should go back to work. Did you call Oxford American back? They want your help putting the new dictionary together, like you did for them before."

Before. She knew that wasn't what Carl originally intended to say. She knew he was going to say *like you did for them ten years ago* and she knew why he stopped himself. That it had already been ten years was too much to contemplate. Ten years. Billy hadn't even lived that long; he'd come up shy by two.

"No," she said. "I don't think I can do that." Oxford American was where they had stared at her, asked if she was okay, if there was anything they could do. She couldn't be around that. She couldn't keep telling them no, as in *no, I'm not okay* and *no, there's nothing you can do*. She couldn't go back and live through that again.

"Something else, then," Carl said. He looked over the deck railing. "You used to love gardening."

Joyce looked down at the ruins of the garden that had once given her so much joy. How could she make something grow after losing Billy? Surely she would kill everything she touched, passing along the virus of sorrow and pain like a disease. Would it even be right to bring new life to their home?

"Maybe," she said, but she didn't know if she spoke the word to Carl or herself.

Often, at night, Billy sat at the foot of their bed. Sometimes he was the man he would have grown up to be; sometimes he was the eight-year-old child who was taken from them. Once, Joyce poked Carl awake and told him.

"You're just dreaming," he said, holding her tight. "Go back to sleep."

No, she thought. This part is the dream. When I wake up, it will be 1984 again. I'm sitting in the rocking chair, holding the baby to my breast, sleeping. Having a nightmare.

The thought of gardening stayed with her. Maybe Carl was right, maybe she needed something to keep her busy. The Brooklyn Heights Garden Center was only a short walk away. It couldn't hurt to look around.

The chalkboard outside the store read, "Autumn is coming! Check out our selection of midsummer and fall perennials!"

Perennial. Adjective. Lasting a long time or forever.

Had it really been ten years since she last worked with Oxford American? It seemed like just yesterday she helped edit the 1992 edition. And then A.J. Sutton—murderer, molester, destroyer of worlds—appeared out of nowhere and took her Billy-Toad from her. And that was the end of everything.

No boy should only live eight years. Eight years was not a long time, not even close to forever.

Inside, she walked past a crowd of Billys standing by the potted flowers. She tried not to look at them. The woman behind the counter also wore Billy's face, and when she asked if Joyce needed any help she just kept walking.

The aisle marked "Perennials" was on the other side of the store. Joyce looked at the bags of bulbs, wondering what to get. The pictures on the labels all looked so beautiful, but none of them felt right. None of them felt *important* enough.

What was she looking for? She didn't know. She didn't even know if she'd really start gardening again, but it felt good to look. It brought back the memory of rough gardening gloves on her hands, her fingers wrapped around the trowel handle, digging in the soil, planting bulbs, pulling up weeds. It almost made her smile.

Billy appeared next to her and told her not to hesitate to ask if she needed any help, that's what he was there for. He wore a red apron and a nametag: Felicity.

Felicity. Noun. Being happy.

She blinked her eyes twice, and Billy turned into a plump woman with curly brown hair and twinkling eyes. Joyce thanked her and turned away, grabbing the next bag of bulbs off the shelf.

And she knew she'd found the right one.

Tricyrtis Formosana.

The toad lily.

On the label: "A very unusual shade loving perennial with small but eye-catching orchid-like flowers in different shades of purple-blue and white. Midsummer to fall flowering. 3 plants per bag. Suitable for zones 4-8."

Long ago, she knew what those zones meant, knew which zone her own garden was in. Somewhere in her mind, under the blanket of numbing grief, the knowledge was still there, waiting to be used again. Could she do it? Joyce was suddenly frightened. What if she'd lost her green thumb? What if the plants died on her, just like—

She took a deep breath, let the thought go, and looked at the picture on the label. The lily's flat green leaves looked soft, like Billy's hair when she ran her hand through it and called him her little Billy-Toad. The flowers were tall and looked almost pink in the photo; pink like Billy's cheeks when he came home from school on a cold winter day, huffing under his fuzzy blue Giants hat, his green scarf hiding so much of his face all she could see were his eyes, his runny nose, and those cheeks, those apple cheeks.

The sign on the shelf read, "One bag $4.95. Three bags $12.95."

She took six.

Turned to go.

And froze at the mouth of the aisle.

Impossible. Impossible!

Joyce ducked back into the aisle and peeked out over a pyramid display of Miracle-Gro boxes. It was him, standing at the checkout, placing two large bags of mulch on the counter. She blinked once, twice, three times, certain it was another daydream. It *had* to be.

A.J. Sutton. He smiled at the woman behind the counter, a smile that hid the monster, the destroyer of worlds.

How could this be? How could he be out of jail after only ten years? But there was no mistaking that face, she knew it as well as she knew her own: staring day after day in the courtroom at the monster who took Billy from her, the constant news coverage, showing his arrest again and again. *"Seven known victims…boys between the ages of six and ten…Brooklyn Heights playground…guilty plea…life in prison…"*

He shouldn't be out. He *couldn't* be out. It had to be another of her waking dreams.

"As usual, I'll need these delivered," he said. "You've got my address on file already."

That voice!

Joyce waited until he was out of the store before coming out of her hiding place. When she put the bulbs down on the counter, the picture on the labels had changed. She turned away, couldn't look her son in the face.

She didn't tell her psychiatrist about seeing A.J. Sutton at the store. He would just tell her not to give any power to the hallucinations, to let it go. She didn't tell Carl, either. She was just seeing things again, that's all. A.J. Sutton was in jail for life.

The toad lilies wouldn't grow in her garden. She weeded, she watered, she aerated…nothing. She put out poison for the squirrels she suspected might be trying to eat the bulbs, but they still wouldn't grow. She returned to the garden center again and again, buying plant food and fertilizer and even a new hose in case the old one had grown moldy and was spraying toxic water. She went so many times they began to know her by name. Felicity and the woman behind the counter, Gretchen, always smiled and said, "Hi, Joyce. Nice to see you again."

And Joyce would say, "I need a new aeration fork, mine's rusty and might be affecting the plants," or, "I need to try a different kind of plant food, the last one's not working," or, "Do you think mulch would help?"

Nothing worked. The toad lilies didn't come up. There should have been shoots by now, tough little greens poking up from the earth, but there was only defiance, mockery, an empty space that said *everything you love will be taken from you, everything you touch will die.*

Frustrated, angry, Joyce stabbed the soil with her hand trowel, over and over. "Grow, God damn you! Why won't you grow?"

Grow for Billy! If not for me, then for Billy!

Carl raced out the back door and was kneeling in the dirt with his arms around her before she knew it. She sobbed, and Carl rocked her back and forth.

"I'm sorry!" she screamed into his shirt. "I'm sorry!"

"Maybe you just need some compost to help them along," Felicity said. "Do you have a compost bin at home?"

From the corner of her eye, Joyce saw Billy leaning against the wall of the store. She tried to resist turning and looking, but couldn't. It was just a rake, pale wood and green metal, nothing more. She hadn't seen Billy in a long time. Her psychiatrist said she was making real progress. She didn't know how to feel about seeing Billy again.

"Maybe I need a new bin," she said.

Felicity led her to the proper aisle and showed her the new plastic compost bins with snap-lock lids, heavy-duty handles, wheels on the bottom. They all looked so clean and nice, nothing like the rotted wooden mess Joyce had in the corner of her garden.

"We can deliver it to you," Felicity said. "It's a free service after five o'clock."

Joyce paid by credit card and walked out of the store. Halfway down the block, she turned around and headed back, realizing she'd forgotten to tell them she wouldn't be at home after six because she and Carl had dinner plans.

She gasped when she saw A.J. Sutton pulling open the door of the garden center. It *was* him, there was no doubt about it this time. Her mind had grown clearer over the past weeks; the hallucinations were happening less often.

But could she be so sure? Hadn't she just seen Billy in the store today?

A rake, a goddamn rake, of all things!

No, this was different. It was him all right. She'd know that face anywhere. A.J. Sutton was a free man. Only ten years for taking her Billy-Toad from her and countless other Billy-Toads from their mothers. Ten years and out on the street doing who knows what, as if nothing had happened, as if he weren't a monster in human skin, as if he were the King of Brooklyn Heights, untouchable, unaccountable. That wasn't right. That wasn't right at all.

She turned and saw for the first time a sign in the shop's window.

HELP WANTED.

"I got a job," Joyce said.

"You're kidding," Carl said. "That's great!"

"I'm working at the garden center. I start tomorrow."

"I'm so proud of you," Carl said.

She smiled and leaned against him. Billy would have been proud of her, too.

Days passed and still the toad lilies stayed underground. She nurtured them anyway, watering them, feeding them compost from everything she put in the new plastic bin: egg shells, the remains of turkey dinners, coffee grounds, dead leaves, grass clippings. The compost was rich and dark, there were even worms in it now, helping break it all down into useable plant food, but still it didn't make the lilies grow. It occurred to her that maybe the bulbs were dead. With her employee discount, it would be easy to buy some more, but she wanted *these* bulbs to grow. If she had to bring them back from the dead, then that's what she would do.

Days passed and Billy showed himself to her less and less. Lampposts stayed lampposts, elderly Korean women in floral dresses remained themselves, children on buses wore their own faces. Sometimes she thought she saw him sitting at the foot of the bed and saying, "You know what you need to do," but even that was becoming rare, and she always knew she was dreaming when it happened. Her psychiatrist said she was doing great. Carl said she was almost her old self again.

Days passed and still A.J. Sutton did not return to the Brooklyn Heights Garden Center. It frustrated her, and when she got too upset she'd inevitably see Billy again in passing taxis, the subway, the audience of a movie theater.

But she was patient, too. She was nothing if not patient.

Then Carl's father got sick, and he had to leave. "Maybe just a few weeks," Carl said. "Maybe a month. I don't know yet. Mom needs help. Are you sure you don't want to come along?"

"I'm sure," she said. "I should stay here."

Carl was disappointed, but he said he understood. He might have been lying. She didn't know, didn't really care. It wasn't a priority right now.

The day Carl flew to Wyoming, A.J. Sutton came into the store.

They were closing for the night when Gretchen said, "Only one delivery this evening."

"I'll do it," Joyce said. "Carl's away, so I don't have to rush home."

"Fine by me," Felicity said, locking the front door. "I'd love to get home early."

"Done," Gretchen said. She handed a jangling key ring to Joyce. "Take the SUV, we've got five bags of mulch for Mr. Sutton today."

"More mulch?" Felicity asked. "What the hell is in that guy's garden?"

I have some ideas, Joyce thought, but she kept her mouth shut.

While Gretchen and Felicity were in back counting out the register drawers, Joyce dragged the mulch bags to the front door. Then she went back into the aisles and grabbed a few more items from her own list.

The address on the order slip was a building on the corner of Willow and Clark, not far from the store at all. Just a short drive in Gretchen's SUV. It was a big car. There would be enough room.

In the rearview mirror, she thought she saw Billy sitting in the back seat. She thought he was smiling at her.

The order slip said to press buzzer number one. The only name on the buzzer was "Superintendent." Joyce, standing before the door to the apartment building and wondering just what the hell she was doing, looked around. There was a vast, well-manicured garden in front, with banzai trees, flowering shrubs, and perfectly tailored green grass. Around the base of the plants, the ground was covered with red and brown mulch. It looked beautiful. She was almost jealous.

"You're new," A.J. Sutton said.

He was dressed in stained blue overalls and had dirt on his face. His basement apartment was cramped, musty and hot from the nearby boiler room. A single bed was pushed against one wall. There was a TV on a rolling stand and a recliner with a dinner tray in front of it. The floor was littered with old magazines and fast food wrappers.

Squalid. Adjective. Dirty and unpleasant, especially because of neglect or poverty.

But there was another meaning, too.

Squalid. Adjective. Morally degrading.

A.J. helped her with the mulch bags, piling them between the bed and the TV.

"I just started working there a little while ago," she said.

"I'm A.J." He extended his hand.

She didn't take it. "I know."

"Of course you do. It's on the order." He smiled and let his hand drop. "I take care of the garden outside. One of my many duties here."

"I saw it. It's beautiful."

"Thanks. I learned a lot about gardening when I was...when I was away."

"Oh," she said.

"Yeah." He took a deep breath. "I know this doesn't look like much of a life, but it's helping me keep my head on straight, you know? I've learned a lot about myself, about how people can change. For the better, I mean. Starting over."

"Oh," she said.

Joyce unloaded the shopping bag she'd brought with her from the store: a box of heavy lawn and leaf garbage bags, a pruning saw, hedge clippers.

"Oops," A.J. said. "I didn't order those."

"No," she said.

She opened the box of garbage bags, pulled one out, and spread it on the floor.

"What are you doing?"

"You don't remember me," she said. "I doubt you remember any of us. But you do remember the kids, don't you?"

He looked surprised. "What?"

"We met in court," she said.

It took A.J. a long moment to find his voice. "Yeah, I remember you. I remember them all. I know I can't make it up to you or anyone…"

"Oh," she said, peeling off the plastic wrap on the pruning saw.

"I'm not the same person I was then. I had a lot of anger in me. They helped me work through all that."

Joyce noticed he didn't move, didn't try to stop her or call for help. There was no panic in his voice. Maybe he'd known for a long time now this was coming.

"If I could do anything to take it all back, I would. All I can do is say I'm sorry."

Sorry. Adjective. Feeling pity, regret or sympathy.

But this word, too, had another meaning.

Sorry. Adjective. Wretched.

"I'm sorry I took your son from you," he said.

"Oh," she said.

"Honey?" Carl's voice inside the house.

"I'm in the garden!" she called back. The sun was already starting to drop, casting shadows over the rich soil.

"I missed you," Carl said, coming down the steps from the deck. "Longest goddamn three weeks of my life."

"I'm so glad your father's doing better," Joyce said. She was still kneeling, tending to the plants.

"Will you look at that?" Carl whistled and knelt down beside her, one arm around her shoulders. "I can't believe they finally grew."

She nodded, beaming. The toad lilies stood strong and

proud, their purple and white flowers in full bloom. The whole garden was full of them. "It was worth the wait," she said.

"How, after all this time?"

She shrugged. "I guess they just needed the right kind of compost, that was all."

Carl stood and walked over to the compost bin.

He put his hand on the plastic lid.

"Don't do that," Joyce said, louder than she meant to. Then she gave him a smile to put him at ease. "It just smells something awful in there. Why don't you go unpack, and I'll have dinner ready soon."

"You're incredible." Carl kissed her forehead and went back inside.

Incredible. Adjective. Very surprising.

Yes, that was her all right. Full of surprises.

Joyce, bursting with pride, looked at her toad lilies again.

And the lilies looked back at her, each with Billy's face, Billy's smiling face.

THE JEW OF PRAGUE

I visited Prague with my father and brother in the spring of 1990, shortly after the Berlin Wall came down and the Eastern Bloc collapsed. What stuck with me from that trip were two things: the more than two-decades-old bullet holes that still riddled some of the building facades from when the Soviet Union invaded Czechoslovakia in the late 1960s, and the Old Jewish Cemetery in Josefov. The cemetery really is as crowded as I describe it here. Weaving through the narrow aisles between crammed together tombstones was unlike anything I'd ever experienced. It took my breath away. When the idea for "The Jew of Prague" came to me, I knew I had to make that cemetery an integral part of it. Like "Under the Skin," it's one of the few stories where my Jewish heritage comes to the fore. It's also an early attempt at mixing crime fiction with the supernatural. Some forerunners of General Slocum's Gold can definitely be found here.

November 9, 1989: the Berlin Wall is breached. The collapse of Communism extends like falling dominos throughout Eastern Europe.

December 29, 1989: Czechoslovakia's Communist rule ends after the month-long Velvet Revolution. The borders open.

January 10, 1990: David Malin, in New York, gets the call from Browning.

"This is the chance we've been waiting for, David. We're giving it six months for the political climate to cool down; then you're on a plane to Prague."

Two hours from touchdown at Prague Ruzyne airport, with

the cramped airplane seat taking its toll on his knees, David switched on the overhead light and looked once more at the dossier Browning sent him.

He'd heard countless stories about Karl Sarka—it came with the territory—but he never believed all the hype. "Sarka was the best jewel thief who ever lived," they said. "Sarka stole the Warsaw Opal from right under Hitler's nose," they said. "Sarka could've stolen the ring off Napoleon's hand. He could've stolen the necklace right off Cleopatra's goddamn tits."

The only thing David knew for sure about Karl Sarka was that he was dead. Sarka had the bad luck to be in Czechoslovakia in 1948, when the Communists staged a *coup d'état,* closed the borders, tossed the president out a window, and arrested just about everyone with two legs and a pulse. Caught and killed; that's what being the world's best jewel thief got him.

But not before he stashed the mother lode.

"It's a diamond," Browning had said on the phone back in New York. "About the size of a marble. It may not be the biggest, but it's special, believe me. It's worth millions, and we've got people willing to pay. You'll get a better deal on this one, too. You come back with it, we go fifty-fifty on the sale."

"What's the catch?"

"None. This is the white whale, Davey. This is the one Sarka stashed before the Commies got him."

"Fuck off."

"I'm serious. We're talking the big time here. We're talking the Jew of Prague."

David stepped off the airplane, squinting while his eyes adjusted to the afternoon sunlight. It was June, but the air was mild, not the hazy swelter he'd left back in New York. From the blacktop, Prague Ruzyne airport looked nothing like the international airports he knew—no LaGuardia sprawl, no JFK grime—just a squat, tawny building a couple of blocks wide. Unremarkable.

A banner hung over the arrival entrance. President Havel's smiling face beamed down at him—trim mustache, thick eyebrows, eyes that all but said, "I died for your sins"—welcoming him to *First Summer—Prague 1990*. In English.

At the crowded immigration desk, they barely looked at his passport. The blue-coated officer saw "United States of America" printed on the cover, saw the bald eagle clutching its arrows and leafy branches—saw, ultimately, the tourist dollars it represented—and stamped it right away.

"You know where staying in Prague?" the officer asked. His English was awful.

"Not yet," David said. "I need to be in Josefov. Any hotels there?"

The officer pushed a slick, color brochure across the desk to him: glossy cover photo of a picturesque town square, a tower with a big blue and gold clock, and printed across the top, *Prague Hotel Accommodations*. In English, again.

Barely six months since the borders opened, and they were ready for the tourists.

Josefov, it turned out, had only one available place to stay, a rooming house above the Sametová Revoluce bar on Maiselova street. David was used to better digs—two years ago, when the black market was really cooking, he went after the Ming Necklace in Hong Kong, and Browning put him up at the decadently expensive Mandarin Oriental—but the rooming house would do, and its location was perfect.

Both the bar and the rooms above were owned by some kids fresh out of college, ready to capitalize on the freedom boom. In U.S. dollars, the room was only twenty-five a night. Still cheap. In another six months, it would be five times that.

The room was small, decorated with creaky furniture from the Fifties and faded floral wallpaper that reeked of cigarettes. David hefted his small brown suitcase onto the bed, flipped it open and took out his bathroom kit. He unscrewed the bottom of the empty shaving cream container and pulled out a long piece of metal. He unscrewed the fake shaving razor from the top of its hollow, reinforced handle. He opened the back of his thick wooden hairbrush and pulled out a third piece of metal.

Then he snapped it all together, and strapped the makeshift pistol to his ankle.

From the window, as the sun melted into the horizon, David

could see the Vltava River winding like a black snake in the distance.

And between the river and the rooming house, David could see the cemetery.

"You mean the *Jewel* of Prague," David had said, laughing and tugging on the phone cord. He could see the spire of the Empire State Building from the vast picture windows of his living room. "For a moment, I thought you said—"

"I did," Browning said.

David frowned. "Funny name for a diamond."

"That's what makes it so special. There's a flaw, right in the center, that's the exact replica of an *aleph*."

"The fuck's an *aleph*?"

"It's a Hebrew letter, numbskull. How do you not know this? You're one of them, aren't you?"

"Only by birth," David said. "So how come I've never heard of this stone?"

"It's before your time, kiddo," Browning said. "Back in the Forties, it was kept in the Czech Army Museum, but legend says it goes back to the days of Rudolf the Second, when it was given to him by the Jews because he was so nice to them or something. Sarka pinched it from the Army Museum, but then the Commies got him. This thing's like the Holy Grail now. Everyone wants it, and everyone knows it's still in Prague, just where Sarka left it."

"So where'd he leave it?"

"The Old Jewish Cemetery in Josefov."

"No problem."

"Sure," Browning said. "No problem. You've only got twelve thousand graves to go through."

Even at night, without the sun baking Prague's industrial pollution into stew, the city smelled worse than New York. Decades of environmental neglect had taken its toll; the air was thick with the stench of petroleum and smog. Back home, David could stand behind a bus and get fresher air.

He crossed Maiselova toward the cemetery, instinctively

avoiding the cones of light shining down from the curved street lamps. A few couples walked hand in hand on the sidewalk, but it was hardly crowded. No one stiffened when they saw him, no one turned away too fast or looked too long, the way someone tailing him would.

A cement wall, black with grime and cracked with age, surrounded the cemetery. It only came up to his shoulders; David could probably jump it, but there were no lights in the cemetery, and an after-hours visitor with a flashlight would attract too much attention. The thick trunks of gnarled black trees formed a barricade just inside the walls; another deterrent. He would have to come back during the day for reconnaissance.

Fading light from the street lamps reached into the cemetery, skimming the tops of the headstones. David couldn't see much, just shapes and silhouettes, but what he saw didn't make his job seem easier. It was like a sea of stone, solid waves jutting up from the darkness at odd angles, some pointed, some rounded, all crammed right next to each other.

Browning said there were twelve thousand graves in the Old Jewish Cemetery. The cemetery itself didn't look that big—he'd seen a bigger one out in Queens, where they buried his grandmother with all the other rich dead Jews from her congregation—but the sheer multitude of graves was off-putting. It would take days to find the right one.

There had to be a better way.

A flash of movement, dark and quick, caught his eye. Just a few yards away, someone ducked around the corner of the cemetery wall.

David turned and walked toward the corner. The hem of his pant leg flapped against the pistol strapped to his ankle. When he turned the corner, no one was there.

Instinct said he was being followed.

His instinct was never wrong.

Two cars passed each other on the road behind him, and three chattering couples strolled past. This was no place for a confrontation.

David turned and walked back toward Maiselova. If he was being followed, he needed to lose them. Returning to his room would be a bad idea, he didn't want to show them where he was staying, so he ducked into the Sametová Revoluce bar downstairs.

It was practically empty. One of the kids he rented the room from was behind the bar, his face lit from below by a light under the bar's glass surface. One table had three men sitting at it, talking quietly in Czech. The other tables were empty.

Two of the walls were covered with murals. On one, Václav Havel. On the other, Franz Kafka.

Only one barstool was occupied: a slim, blonde woman in a white blouse and black slacks sitting at the far end of the bar. David figured she was late-twenties, early-thirties; his age, more or less. She looked up at the door when he entered. The light coming up from the bar flashed off her blue eyes and highlighted the freckles dotting her cheekbones. She smiled politely, and looked back down at the book she was reading.

He would be safe here, for now.

David took a stool at the opposite end of the bar.

"You're the American staying upstairs, right?" the bartender asked. His English was perfect, but the Czech accent was still there.

"David," he said.

"That's right," the bartender said. "I'm Rudolf."

David nodded. "Like the king."

"More like the reindeer," Rudolf said. "What can I get you?"

David ordered a bottle of Pilsner, and asked, "When does the Old Jewish Cemetery open tomorrow?"

The woman at the other end of the bar looked up from her book.

Rudolf pointed a thumb over his shoulder at her. "Hanne's the one you should talk to. She works for the Jewish Museum."

David picked up his beer and went over to sit next to her.

"The Jewish Museum runs the cemetery?" David asked.

"We take care of it," Hanne said. Her accent was thicker than Rudolf's, but her English was just as good.

"God." David shook his head. "That's a lot to take care of. Twelve thousand graves."

Hanne and Rudolf looked at each other and laughed.

"Twelve thousand?" Hanne said. "You've been reading the wrong guidebooks. There may only be that many headstones, but there are a hundred thousand people buried in the cemetery, all packed tight, one on top of the other. They had to close it two hundred years ago, it got so full."

David frowned. Suddenly the job seemed a lot more complicated.

"The cemetery opens at nine tomorrow," Hanne continued. "You can buy tickets at Klauzová Synagóga."

"The Klaus Synagogue," Rudolf explained.

Hanne nodded, an embarrassed smile curling her lips. "Yes. Tickets cost two hundred and fifty *koruna*, but they also get you into almost all the synagogues and the ceremonial hall."

"It's a rip-off," Rudolf said. "It's only that much for tourists. Czechs get in for fifty *koruna*."

Hanne threw a balled-up napkin at him, and called him something in Czech that David couldn't understand.

"Nice talk from such a devoutly religious woman," Rudolf said, tossing the napkin back at her.

"How devout?" David asked her.

"She works for the Jewish Museum," Rudolf said. "What more do you need?"

"You don't look Jewish," David said.

"No?" Hanne said. "What does a Jew look like?"

David shrugged. "I don't know."

"She had a bigger nose before the plastic surgery," Rudolf said.

"Enough," Hanne said, pushing her empty glass toward him. "Another, please." She shifted in her seat, and something clanked in the purse strapped to the back of her chair.

Something that sounded like keys. Big keys.

"Maybe you can help me," David said.

"Maybe," she said.

"I need information about someone buried in the cemetery. Someone important."

"Who?"

When David said the name, Rudolf rolled his eyes up toward the ceiling and said, "Oy!"

Before David left for Prague, Browning called him one last time.

"I told you this thing was the goddamn Holy Grail," Browning said. He sounded angry. "Looks like we're not the only ones planning a trip."

"Who else?" David asked. He wound the phone cord around his fist. In any other business, competition was healthy. In this one, it could get you killed. Since David started working for Browning ten years ago, he'd seen his share of guns pointed at him; but he was a quick draw, and many times that was all that came between him and a coffin. It was never pleasant.

"Leighton," Browning said. "He's got the scent. Word has it he's already on his way to Prague."

"Shit." Leighton was their biggest competitor. A middle-aged, black market legend operating out of Nevada, Leighton was as well known for his collection of priceless Asian gemstones as he was for his ruthless tactics. They'd crossed paths once before. David lost the Mandarin Jade Buddha to him half a year ago, and still had the bullet scar on his thigh to remind him.

"Relax," Browning said, "it'll be okay. We've got the edge, even if he gets there first."

"Yeah? How's that?"

He could almost hear Browning smirking on the other end. "Everyone knows Sarka stashed it in the Old Jewish Cemetery, but we've got information Leighton doesn't have. We know whose grave."

David let go of the phone cord. "How?"

"I work for the same organization Sarka did, way back when. Times change, but things stay the same. They found his letters. They're pretty sure they know the name. I'm sending you a dossier today; it's got all the info in it. Plane tickets, too. You're heading out ASAP."

"Whose grave is it?" David asked.

"Sarka must've had a weird sense of humor. He stashed the Jew of Prague with a dead rabbi. I don't know why, but for some reason Sarka thought it would be safest in that particular grave." The sound of papers rustling, then: "Rabbi Judah Löw ben Bezazel. How's that for a fucking name, huh?"

"Yeah," David said. "We hebes really take the cake."

Hanne met him outside the Pinkas Synagogue at eight in the morning. The synagogue was just two blocks from the rooming house, on Siroká street, right up against one end of the Old Jewish Cemetery. It was a stone building three stories high, with arched windows and a black-shingled roof. Like every other building in Prague, its facade was turning brown from grime and pollution. And like every other building in Prague, its walls were still riddled with bullet holes from the Soviet invasion decades ago.

"Good morning," Hanne said. She had a small, purse-like backpack strapped to her shoulders. Her blouse was red, and cut much lower than what she was wearing at the bar last night. She had a short black skirt instead of slacks. She smiled a little wider, a little longer, than before.

David smiled back, making sure it matched the intensity of hers. "Good morning, Hanne."

"Mr. Nebesky's inside," Hanne said. "He's on the phone right now, but he'll be with you shortly."

"And he can show me the grave?"

She nodded, then led him up the steps toward the arched doorway. "Did you bring a yarmulke?"

The question stunned David. It hadn't even occurred to him. "No," he said, "I didn't."

"You'll need something to cover your head. I'm sure we can find you one inside."

Just past the entrance was a wicker basket on a small table. Hanne reached in and pulled out a black cloth yarmulke. David put it on his head. His hand faltered for a moment.

He hadn't worn a yarmulke in nearly twenty years. Such things just didn't matter to him anymore. He hadn't even worn one at his grandmother's funeral. His entire family attended synagogue every weekend, and they thought he was crazy. They stopped talking to him long ago. Evidently, after he turned down the umpteenth invitation to Shabbat services, they figured there was nothing left to say. It was just as well. As far as he was concerned, they could shove it up their Yiddisher asses. In his line of work, he didn't need family connections holding him back anyway.

Though the synagogue was now the headquarters of the Jewish Museum, and no longer used for worship, she explained that visitors still had to wear yarmulkes. It was still a house of God.

To David's surprise, the stone walls inside were inscribed top to bottom with names and dates, reminding him of the Vietnam Memorial back home.

"There are over seventy thousand names up there," Hanne said. "All victims of the Nazis."

Her hand stroked the open collar of her silk blouse; slowly, as if she didn't even know she was doing it.

In another room, the walls were covered with torn, faded children's drawings behind sheets of glass: stick figure families, barking dogs, men in dark uniforms with guns, and everywhere thick black lines of barbed wire.

"Aren't they amazing?" Hanne said. Her cheeks seemed flushed, her breathing more shallow. "They were drawn by the children at Terezín during the war. A few of those kids made it out alive, and some of them are still around today. Just one or two, I think, but that's really something, isn't it?"

David nodded. "Yeah, that's something."

But that's not what he wanted to say. Inside, he said, "This is what I hate, this stupid fascination with persecution, all this living in the goddamn past." Not out loud, though. That would have blown everything he was working toward. Instead, he smiled and held her gaze, only breaking eye contact when he was certain it would seem a moment too long.

"We're going through here," Hanne said, pointing to a vaulted door marked *Vstup Zakázán*. "This is Mr. Nebesky's office."

It was big for a personal office, maybe eight hundred square feet. Nebesky stood behind a wide wooden desk, a leather office chair pushed up against the wall behind him. He was still on the phone, holding it hard against his ear with a meaty hand. He looked to be in his late fifties, with bushy gray hair, thick lips, heavy eyes, a stomach that pushed past his tight brown belt, and…

The nose.

The Jewish nose David had been spared from by sheer genetic luck. He wouldn't think himself half as handsome if he had that nose. He doubted anyone would.

Nebesky, red-faced, shouted into the phone, "I don't understand. Do you want my business or not?"

Hanne smiled at David and whispered, "It'll just be a moment."

David smiled back, and turned around to look at the wall behind him. It was covered with a large mural, thick oil paint in vibrant colors. He recognized the people in the mural from their appearance: long black coats, wide brimmed black hats, untrimmed beards, long side curls framing their faces.

They were *Hasidim*, the ultra-orthodox Jewish sect. He'd seen them in person only once, on a brief trip out to Borough Park, Brooklyn, to talk to a diamond merchant whose breath stank of herring, and whose wife wasn't allowed to shake his hand.

Frozen in time by the mural's artist, the *Hasidim* prayed aloud from open books, bending and chanting in front of what David recognized as the Wailing Wall in Israel. What he didn't recognize were the small leather boxes strapped to their foreheads.

"*Teffillin*," Hanne explained. "They're hollow inside, and contain scriptural verse on little pieces of paper. To keep God close in time of prayer."

"Then you *don't* want my business?" Nebesky roared into the telephone. "No problem, and fuck you, too." He slammed the receiver down onto the cradle. "Such an ass," he said.

Hanne turned around. "What happened?"

Nebesky ran a hand through his thick hair. "The more things change, the more they stay the same. Now that the Communists are finally gone, everyone's free to hate the Jews again." He looked up, saw David standing there, and extended his hand. "Sorry you had to hear that. Mordechai Nebesky."

"David Malin."

"You're the one looking for Rabbi Löw, yes? You want to see where he's buried?"

"I'd really appreciate it," David said.

They led David out of the office, then through a side door that opened right onto the cemetery. "We don't officially open the cemetery to visitors for another hour," Nebesky said. "But when Hanne told me you were researching a book for a big American publisher, I couldn't refuse. Just remember us when it's time to write those thank-yous, okay?"

Hanne's hand brushed against David's as they walked, and she yanked it away. She smiled at him, just for a moment, then looked down at her feet. The red in her face made her freckles pop out.

In daylight, the Old Jewish Cemetery was overwhelming. The stones were chipped and battered with age, all the same oatmeal brown color. Some had been weathered down to lumpy blankness, while others still had visible traces of Hebrew or a Jewish star.

There were thousands of stones, and no more than six inches between them. In some places, they were right up against each other, shoulder to shoulder like soldiers. Some were so close to their neighbors behind them that the bodies must have been stacked on top of each other. David couldn't even see the ground between them.

"Rabbi Löw lived back in the Sixteenth Century," Nebesky said. "It was a bad time for the Jews. He lived here in Josefov, which at the time was just a walled ghetto, a *shtetl*. There were *pogroms* back then; people coming into the ghetto, killing families and burning homes. Just because they were Jews. They didn't need any other reason. Rabbi Löw was a student of the mystical Kabbalah, and they say he used those teachings to save the ghetto from destruction."

"How?"

Nebesky stopped and turned to face him. "He created the golem."

David blinked in confusion. Hanne smiled at him.

"Rabbi Löw, as legend has it, created a man from the mud of the Vltava River," Nebesky continued, pointing over the cemetery wall at the river in the distance. "He brought the golem to life to protect the ghetto."

"Sounds like voodoo," David said.

"No," Hanne said. "It was a miracle of God that allowed the golem to live, not magic. Life where there was none before. The rabbi wrote the Hebrew word *shem* on a piece of paper and put it in the golem's mouth. That's what brought it to life."

"What does *shem* mean?"

"Translated, it means 'renown,' " Nebesky said. "But it's also the name of Noah's oldest son, and the middle name of the Baal Shem Tov, the founder of Hasidism. No one's sure of the significance."

"But the golem went crazy," Hanne said. "It started attacking the people of the ghetto, and destroying property. Rabbi Löw had to disable it by taking the paper out of its mouth."

"Sounds rough," David said.

"Sometimes you do what you have to do for what's right, no matter what the cost," Hanne said.

"Rabbi Löw is one of the most important historical figures in Czechoslovakian Judaism," Nebesky said. He stopped walking, and pointed. "That's why he gets such a special place in the cemetery."

And there it was, marked by a pair of small marble obelisks on either side: the grave of Rabbi Löw. It was slightly taller than the surrounding headstones, but most of its carvings had weathered away. No other graves crowded it; no one was buried on top of him.

Sarka's mother lode, right under David's feet. It gave him goosebumps just thinking about it.

Nebesky took a deep breath. "They say the rabbi was so holy, so loved by God, that his body remains uncorrupted in his grave. But he's so revered, who would dare dig him up to see if that's true?"

Nebesky laughed. So did David, but for a different reason.

David knelt down in front of the headstone, pretending to get a better look. He slipped a small electronic device from his sleeve and let it drop to the ground. They didn't notice.

After David promised to return tomorrow to take some

pictures, Nebesky went back inside, and Hanne led David along the cemetery path to the main gate. She kept smiling at him, then looking away when he caught her.

She pulled a large key ring out of her backpack. David watched as she slipped one into the padlock. The keys made a familiar clanking noise.

"Hanne," David said, "if you're free, maybe we could meet up later? Get some dinner?" He took off the yarmulke and handed it back to her. He made sure his fingers touched hers, just for a moment.

"I'd like that," Hanne said, smiling even wider. "I know a place."

On the other side of the gate, as Hanne locked it behind him and shouted goodbye again, the tourists were already lining up to get in. There were dozens of them, the line extending all the way along the cemetery wall. Near the back of the crowd, a man with spiky green hair saw David, froze, then bolted.

David's instincts kicked in. This was his shadow; this was the man who followed him last night.

David ran after him, past the line of chattering tourists, but lost him on the crowded street. A tour group of almost a hundred people swarmed toward the cemetery, speaking German and filling the entire road. David stopped, trying to spot his shadow again. There, bobbing up for a split second from the sea of heads, a flash of green.

David took off, weaving through the crowd, feeling the pistol dig into his ankle as he ran. Another flash of green, a pair of anxious eyes glancing back to see if David was still there, and then all bets were off. David's green-haired shadow started, shoved people aside, pushing loudly through the crowd. David did the same.

A dark opening appeared between the buildings on the next block: an alley. The green-haired man ran into the approaching crowd of sightseers on that block, then disappeared.

It didn't take a genius to figure it out.

David stopped at the mouth of the alley, crouching low and silently catching his breath. When the sightseers passed, he reached under his pant leg and unstrapped the pistol. Then, on the count of three, he whipped himself around the corner into the dim light of the alley.

A mountain of black trash bags was piled near the back wall. A green spot stuck out.

"You know," David said, "if you don't want to be seen, maybe you should change your hair color."

The green spot didn't move.

"Come on," David said. "Are you really that stupid?"

Two hands popped into the air from behind the bags, then the rest of him emerged slowly. David got a good look at him for the first time. He was just a kid; nineteen, maybe twenty. He looked like he was going to piss his pants.

David motioned with his gun. The green-haired man stepped over the garbage and came forward, muttering, "Shit."

"What's your name, kid?" David asked.

"Andre."

"You've been following me."

"They said you know where the diamond is. They said to follow you."

"Who's *they*?"

Andre kept his mouth shut.

"If you talk, maybe I won't shoot," David said.

Andre stared at the gun in David's hand. "Mr. Leighton sent me," he said. His chin quivered.

David nodded. "You tell *Mr.* Leighton if he wants to find me, he should do it himself, not send some punk asshole kid in his place. You tell him that for me."

David turned around and walked toward the mouth of the alley. He knew better than to put his gun away.

"Hey, asshole," Andre said. The kid tried to sound like someone who knew what he was doing. It was almost cute.

David spun around. Andre pulled a stubby handgun from his belt. Taurus PT-940, double action, all steel and vigor; too much muscle for such a stupid kid.

David shot first. Maybe he only had a spring-loaded pistol snapped together from custom-made pieces of metal, but he'd always been a quick draw, and that mattered more. Andre collapsed, falling backward onto the pile of garbage bags.

David glanced back at the entrance, making sure the shot hadn't attracted attention. No one was there, just a shaft of light from the climbing sun.

"That was dumb," David said, walking over to Andre. The kid was holding his left hand against his gut, a red stain seeping through the shirt under his palm. His teeth were clenched and bare. There was blood in his mouth. "All you had to do was pass on a simple message."

"Fuck you, old man," Andre said, dribbling red onto his chin.

He didn't expect it to, but that stung him a little. *Old man.* David was maybe ten years older than Andre, but suddenly it seemed as if there were whole generations between them. Had he ever been so young, so stupid?

Andre still had the gun in his right hand. He tried to lift it, his arm shaking.

David raised his pistol. A bullet to the head, and it was, "See you in hell, kid."

It didn't take much effort to gain Hanne's trust: some dinner, some drinks. She laughed in all the right places, and touched his arm whenever she could. When she showed him the Fifteenth Century astronomical clock in the old Town Square, her hand brushed against his. This time, she didn't pull it away.

She said, "Why is it that so many Jews in America act like their history and their traditions don't matter, all in the name of assimilation? It's like they're still hiding in Babylon."

David wasn't really listening; he didn't care about anything she was talking about, though he made sure to agree with everything she said, going so far as to tell her how important Jewish tradition was to him.

After that, it was easy getting Hanne to come back with him to his room. She talked the whole way there.

"Wasn't that a weird story, about the golem?" she said. "Do you really think you could bring an inanimate object to life like that?"

David shrugged, gleefully imagining Leighton's reaction to the news about Andre.

"If Rabbi Löw's body is really still uncorrupted after all this time," she said, "would that mean *all* the stories are true?"

"Maybe," David said, thinking about his plan to get the diamond, and then get the hell out of Prague before Leighton had a chance to make his move.

For such a religious woman, Hanne didn't seem to have any problems with sex. She kissed him the moment they entered his room. David didn't even have time to open the bottle of wine he carried from the bar downstairs. She backed him onto the bed, and only stopped kissing him to unbutton his shirt.

For all her assertiveness just minutes before, Hanne was surprisingly shy in bed. For some reason, David thought this was sweet, and that caught him off guard. She wanted him to hold her afterward, and the feel of her naked back, so smooth against his chest, almost made him smile.

But his eyes stayed on her purse, lying where she'd dropped it on the floor.

Hanne got up to use the bathroom.

When she came back, David said, "Do you have to go?"

She nodded. "I have to get home. My mother will worry if I stay out too late."

That she still lived with her mother surprised him, but he didn't ask her about it. No more delays. He got out of bed while she dressed, kissed her once more, and locked the door behind her.

David reached under his pillow and pulled out the prize.

Hanne's heavy keys clanked in his hand.

Half past midnight on a weekday, and the streets of Prague were deserted. Dressed neck to shoes in opaque black, an ebony backpack slung over his shoulder, David slipped around the street lamps and crossed over to the Old Jewish Cemetery. He made his way to the main gate, and tried all the keys on the ring until the padlock sprang open. He pulled the gate open, praying the hinges wouldn't squeak, and slipped inside.

In his gloved fist, David carried a small transmitter. He pressed the button with his thumb, and the tiny device he left at Rabbi Löw's grave blinked brightly at him, showing him the way.

He knelt in front of the headstone and opened his backpack. He took out a small, directional halogen lantern and set it on the ground next to him. He was deep enough inside the cemetery to be sure no one passing by would see the light. Then he pulled out a steel shovelhead, extended the telescoping handle from its base, and went to work.

The old bullet wound in his thigh flared up as he shoveled, but it didn't take long; the bodies here weren't buried deep, though the earth was tight and hard. A flash of dirty white appeared below, and David did the rest with his hands, unearthing something long and thin wrapped in the tattered remains of a sheet.

He unwrapped it like a gift; slowly, gently.

It caught him by surprise.

To say the rabbi's body lay uncorrupted in his grave was not entirely true, but there was no good reason for a three-hundred-year-old corpse *not* to be dust. The gray skin was stretched taut and dry, but it was still there, as were the rabbi's beard, hair, and exceptionally long fingernails. The eyelids were closed, sunk deep into the empty sockets. Only strands remained of the clothes he was buried in, but his yarmulke was intact, as was the shawl around his bony shoulders.

There was no sign of the diamond.

Grimacing, David patted down the body, even parted the teeth of the lipless mouth, but found nothing. He was close to panicking, wondering if Sarka had lied, if all this was for nothing.

His breath caught in his throat when he noticed the small leather box strapped to the corpse's forehead, and suddenly remembered Hanne's words back in Nebesky's office.

Teffillin. They're hollow inside.

David let his breath out slowly.

He pulled the leather box off the rabbi's forehead—some of the sticky gray skin peeled off with it like old glue—and opened it. There was no scripture inside, nothing to bring the rabbi closer to God.

There was only the Jew of Prague.

He held the diamond up to his face, and laughed in spite of

himself. It was real, and it was worth a fortune. He lifted the lantern, and held the diamond in front of it. At its center, he could see the reddish flaw.

So that was an *aleph*. It looked like a stylized letter N, reminding him more of the New York Mets logo than anything else. But something inside him, buried deep and untended, recognized it for it what it was, remembered the Hebrew letter from his Bar Mitzvah lessons a lifetime ago.

It was an uncomfortable memory, and he shrugged it off. All that mattered now was Browning's promise of a fifty-fifty split.

A bright flashlight beam came out of nowhere, illuminating the stone in his hand.

"The Jew of Prague," someone said behind him.

David turned around, his heart pounding. The beam was in his eyes, but he recognized the voice long before his vision adjusted.

"Hanne," he said. He put the lantern down, and let his free hand drift toward the hem of his pant leg.

She took a step forward. "You used me," she said. "Did you really think I wouldn't notice the keys were gone? You used me just to get to this."

David's fingers slid under the hem of his pant leg, and touched cool metal.

"I'm sorry, Hanne," he told her. "But it's like you said, you do what you have to do, no matter what the cost."

"This is entirely different!" she shouted. "The diamond belongs in the Jewish Museum, not in some jewel thief's stash!"

"I'm sorry, Hanne," he said again. He unstrapped the pistol from his leg, and raised it toward her. "I really am."

Hanne's eyes widened, and she took a tentative step back. "You're going to shoot me?" Her voice was unsteady.

David touched the trigger, and swallowed hard.

Memory's a funny thing. It can fill an empty moment with happiness, or it can curse you with regret. It can change everything in a heartbeat. It can stop you harder than a bullet.

David could feel her in his arms again, as if none of this were happening, as if they were still back in the room; her lips against his, and the cool touch of her skin. He *felt* her sweetness, *felt* how shy she became once their clothes were off and the warm blanket enveloped them; and later, his arms draped over hers from behind, and the only sound the rhythm of their breath.

"Please," Hanne said. "It belongs here, at the museum. You know it does. It belongs with its people."

David let go of the trigger. The pistol only held five bullets, and he'd used two of them already on the green-haired kid. He might need the others later. There was no sense in wasting them here, on Hanne.

That's what he told himself, because it was easier that way.

He lowered the gun. "A deal's a deal," he said. "I have to take this with me."

"We'll make a new deal," Hanne said. "We've been looking for it, too, for a long time now. We can pay you for it. You can split it with the detective we hired."

David frowned. "Detective?"

"Hiya, kid." He walked out of the darkness and into the beam of Hanne's flashlight. A tall man, chunky, middle-aged, with a horseshoe of white hair around his bald head, and eyes that flashed blue even in the darkness. One hand was hidden in the pocket of his overcoat. He smiled, and said, "How's your leg?"

David stood up, whipping the pistol forward again. His breath came in anxious bursts.

"Hanne," David said, "get away from him."

"You shouldn't have killed Andre," Leighton said.

"He didn't leave me much choice," David said.

Hanne looked from one to the other. "What are you two talking about? David, put down that gun before someone gets hurt."

"Hanne, get away from him," David said again. "He's not who you think he is. He wants the diamond for himself."

"Stop it!" Hanne shouted. "We hired him to help us find the Jew of Prague."

"He conned you," David said. "He has buyers waiting for it back in the States, just like I do. People who can pay a *lot* more than your little museum can afford."

The edges of Leighton's smile dropped ever so slightly. His

blue eyes turned to Hanne. David's finger tensed on the trigger.

With one arm, Leighton grabbed Hanne and held her in front of him, his hand over her mouth. Hanne dropped the flashlight to the ground. Its beam spilled past David's legs and illuminated Rabbi Löw's well-preserved face.

With his other arm, Leighton pulled a thick, black handgun from his pocket.

"I don't have time for this," Leighton said, his body hidden behind Hanne's, his face right next to hers. He pointed the gun at David. "Give me the diamond."

David glanced back and forth, from Leighton to Hanne. Hanne's eyes were wide with fear. David had no clear shot.

"No time for dawdling," Leighton said. "You're in way over your head, kid. You've only been doing this, what, ten years now? Browning must have recruited you right out of college. You're still just an amateur. Give it to me, and everything ends okay."

David looked at Hanne again. He wanted his arms to move, to drop the gun, to hand over the diamond, but they stayed where they were, as if they knew better.

Leighton pulled the trigger. The bullet ricocheted off Rabbi Löw's headstone, knocking out a small chunk of rock, and spraying gravel-dust into the beam of David's lantern. Hanne whimpered under Leighton's beefy hand.

"Next shot goes in your head, Malin," Leighton said.

Then he cried out suddenly. A thin rivulet of blood trickled from his hand where Hanne sank her teeth into it.

She broke away from him, but Leighton grabbed her by her collar and brought the butt of his gun down hard on the back of her head. Hanne grunted and fell to the ground.

David squeezed off a shot, but Leighton was fast for his age, as fast as David remembered. Leighton twisted, ducked aside, and David's shot only pierced his flapping overcoat.

David rolled, making for cover behind Rabbi Löw's headstone. A bullet whizzed past him as he moved, and he heard it thud into the ground near him. He stayed behind the headstone, catching his breath.

"You've gotten better since last time," Leighton said. David could hear Leighton's footsteps, slow, cautious, as he crept closer. "I should've killed you when I took the Jade Buddha. Live and learn, huh?"

David still had the Jew of Prague in his left hand. In his right, a gun with only two bullets left. He'd have to make them count.

He somersaulted away from the grave, and leapt to his feet, his finger on the trigger—

A flash from Leighton's gun blinded him.

The smell of gun smoke.

A bullet punched through David's chest and buried itself in his heart.

David fell backward. Both the diamond and the gun dropped out of his hands.

There was no pain, but he felt very sleepy. He had trouble keeping his eyes open as Leighton towered over him. He watched Leighton bend down and picked up the diamond. Leighton's lips moved, but all David could hear was his own ragged breathing.

When David was a boy, his parents owned a slide projector. The family spent hours watching slides from trips to Israel, Europe and Disney World. David was transfixed by the magic of it all: the bright images coming out of that bulky humming box and splashing onto the folding white screen in their living room, the satisfying click of the advance button under his father's thumb, the way the screen would go black between slides, then open up again in full color with a new picture.

It was like watching one of those slide shows now. Black, picture, black, picture.

He saw the silhouette of a man in an overcoat quickly dumping dirt back into a hole in the ground.

He saw Leighton's back from above, and knew he was being carried somewhere.

He thought he heard a car door slam, thought he heard an engine.

He saw a bridge lit by lampposts in the dead of night, black statues lining the bridge's edge. Then David saw the water below. He thought he felt Leighton tying something to his leg, but he couldn't be sure. He was so very sleepy.

Hot breath on his ear. In a voice a million miles away, Leighton said, "See you in hell, kid."

Then the water rushed up to meet him, the last picture of the slideshow. It wasn't cold. He didn't even feel it.

David's body sank like a stone and settled in the mud at the bottom of the Vltava River.

The dry, cracked mud was all over him, caking him head to foot. It was like walking in heavy armor; every step was difficult.

Hanne walked next to him, a square white bandage on the back of her head. It was dark out, but he didn't know if it was the same night or the next, or a thousand nights later.

He looked at his hands as he walked. The mud was brown, gritty, and he could see his skin showing here and there, pale under the streetlamps by the river. He tried to bend his fingers, but it was difficult.

"Here," Hanne said. They turned onto a cobbled side street, and she pointed to a small, one-level house. "He's in there."

He walked up the steps to the front door, knocked it off its hinges, and stepped into the foyer.

Leighton came running around the corner, gun in hand. Then Leighton froze, his mouth hanging slack in confusion, and said, "Didn't I kill you yet?"

He walked toward Leighton. The gun fired. A bullet punched through the mud and into his gut. He didn't care.

Leighton turned and ran into the bedroom. He followed.

"You're not getting the diamond from me," Leighton said, holding up the gun. "Why don't you go home and take a shower?"

He walked toward Leighton. Hanne appeared behind him in the doorway.

"Wait," she said.

He stopped, though he didn't want to. He wanted to pound Leighton into a flat red stain.

"Mr. Leighton," Hanne said, "where's the diamond?"

"So now you two are working together?"

"You do what you have to do for what's right," she said. "No matter what the cost."

"I should've killed you, too," Leighton snarled.

"Take care of him," Hanne said. "I'll find the diamond."

He advanced on Leighton again.

Leighton fired once more, hitting him in the shoulder. He shrugged it off, too angry to care.

"What's wrong with you?" Leighton cried. He shot again, hitting him in the chest. Watery blood trickled out, mixing with the mud.

It didn't matter to him. All that mattered was killing this son of a bitch.

"What's wrong with you?" Leighton screamed it this time.

He snatched the gun from Leighton's hand and tossed it aside. Then he grabbed Leighton's throat, and squeezed. Leighton's legs kicked at him, briefly, then stopped.

He squeezed Leighton's neck so hard that, when Leighton's trachea snapped, so did his own thumb. He let Leighton's limp body drop to the floor.

"Here it is," Hanne said, a square metal box in her hands. She opened it, and the Jew of Prague glittered under the bedroom light. "You have no idea what it means to the Jewish Museum to have this in its collection after all this time. Thank you, David."

Hanne closed the box, walked over to him, and kissed him on the cheek.

"*Shem*," she said.

He opened his mouth for her.

Hanne reached under his tongue and pulled out the piece of paper.

COMEBACK

I've only written two pieces of erotica to date, and oddly both of them have found more success than any of my horror short stories. The first, "V.I.P. Room," was reprinted in Maxim Jakubowski's Mammoth Book of Best New Erotica, Vol. 3. Remarkably, "Comeback" did even better. Aside from first appearing in Fishnet, the premier erotica website for quite a few years, it was reprinted in Susie Bright's The Best American Erotica 2007 and her omnibus anthology X: The Erotic Treasury. An excerpt of the story was even reprinted on Playboy's website in a feature on erotic fiction. In the end, though, I owe it all to Polly Frost. The idea for "Comeback" came to me while I was attending a live reading of one of her erotic soap opera scripts in New York City. As I recall, a character mentioned something about shaving her pubic hair, and from that one offhand comment the idea for "Comeback" sprang almost fully formed into my mind.

The big shindig was at Bruce Glasser's house in Tarzana, the only part of the Valley I don't consider a shithole. It's the same house where we shot a lot of my movies when it belonged to Ricky Samson, owner of Luscious Video back in the Eighties. The *Virgin High* series had turned Bruce into one of the biggest adult film producers in the country, making him rich enough to buy it when Ricky died from screwing the wrong junkie. (Ricky always liked it bareback, and everyone knew it would get him in trouble one day, either dead or a daddy.) It was weird being there for a party instead of a shoot. I kept expecting the doorbell to ring and the late, great Johnny Calzone to come in dressed

like that fucking pizza delivery boy from *Who Ordered Sausage?*
I still can't believe that's the role that got him famous. Though
I guess I'm still best known for playing a high school girl who
fucks her gym teacher on the parallel bars, so maybe I shouldn't
talk.

Bruce only invited me to the party because he was giving
me a role in his newest film, mostly out of pity, I suppose, but
I wasn't about to say no. It's hard being a former starlet who's
crossed to the other side of forty. Everyone thinks you're too
ancient to be in their movies anymore, or you're only good for
the granny porn sites, so I'd mostly been doing dub work on
Japanese anime, the ones where girls get fucked by demons or
whatever. The money's all right, but the job's kind of limiting.
There are only so many ways to make that surprised gasping
noise when the tentacles come out of nowhere and Little Miss
Wide Eyes gets one in every hole.

I felt like a visitor from another planet standing there in
Bruce's crowded living room. Everyone knew everyone else,
they all had their arms around each other and were laughing
at private jokes, but I didn't recognize anyone. A whole new
generation of filmmakers had sprung up since the last time I
was there. I guess I'd expected to sign at least a few cocktail
napkins—*Stay tight! Love, Amber Fox*, just like in the old days
when everyone asked me to sign video boxes—but no one
seemed to remember me, or if they did, they didn't give a shit. I
was just some old lady to them, not worth their attention when
there were so many young hotties in the room.

I flashed for a moment on Jay, my ex-boyfriend, the night he
packed his bags and took off, our two-year relationship dead all
of a sudden because he'd found someone else. Someone younger.
Standing at my door, confused and hurt, I caught a glimpse of her
as Jay tossed his suitcases in the back of his Ford Expedition. Just
a slim, tanned arm poking out of the passenger's side window,
the tattoo of a daisy on her shoulder, her fingers decorated with
silver rings. Not a wrinkle or an ounce of fat on that arm, just the
smooth, golden skin of a twenty-something beach bunny. Inside
the car, the round tip of a cigarette glowed, briefly revealing an
orange-tinted hint of a button nose and curly hair before it faded.

A high-pitched squeal pulled me out of my memories. "Amber?" A girl I'd never seen before ran up to me. She was a skinny, tiny thing with big blonde hair, tight bellbottom jeans and a cropped t-shirt that barely covered her melon chest. She didn't look more than eighteen.

"The one and only," I said, perking up a bit. It's an old joke. Half the women in the biz call themselves Amber.

"Oh my God!" she shrieked, giving me a peek at the metal stud through her tongue. "Amber Fox, I can't believe it!"

"In the flesh," I said. I was relieved someone had finally recognized me, even if she was probably one of the younger stars I'd been losing roles to for the past six years. I tried not to look at how toned and tight her stomach was, but the glittery string of diamonds dangling from her pierced bellybutton kept drawing my eye back. I felt like a whale all of a sudden, so I sucked in my gut and made a mental note to avoid the hors d'oeuvres table for the rest of the night.

"You have no idea how big a fan I am!" she cried, her eyes wide and crazy-looking.

"You'll just have to tell me then," I said, laughing my party laugh. Behind her, someone spread lines of coke on the coffee table. Suddenly it felt like no time had passed—it was still 1986 and I was the hottest adult film actress this side of Seka.

"I'm Krystal Lynn," she said, extending one remarkably tiny hand. Her nails, though, were enormous and had green dollar signs stenciled onto the white polish. I winced in sympathy for any guy unlucky enough to get a handjob from her. "Maybe you saw me in *Ready, Willing and Anal 5*? I won an AVN Award for that. Best Ass to Mouth."

"Congratulations," I said, shaking her hand. "I have an AVN myself."

"I know, Lifetime Achievement!" Krystal squealed. "I know, like, everything about you. You're my hero. You're totally why I got into the business."

I grinned. "Really?"

"*Totally!* My father had, like, *all* your videos. I found them under the sink in his bathroom, and this one time when he was out of town I invited over all my friends from school and we had an Amber Fox marathon. You were *so* cool."

Her *father*? She might as well have stabbed me in the heart. Sometimes I forget how long ago the Eighties were.

She turned around and shouted into the crowd, "Hey, Terry, get your ass over here! You gotta meet someone!" A tall, chunky man closer to my age than hers, with a fuzzy handlebar mustache, a ponytail sticking out the back of his trucker cap, and a big blue knapsack slung over one shoulder, made his way over to us. "This is Amber Fox."

"Yeah?" he said. Not hi, not pleased to meet you, just yeah. "Terry Left. I own Sunset Auto Parts." He said it like I ought to be impressed, then shook my hand with an overly strong grip. I knew his type immediately: the small-time, loud-mouth loser who'd managed to catch a hot, young pornstar girlfriend with daddy issues and thought it made him big shit. I knew the type because that was every boyfriend I'd ever had. They drove me crazy, but sometimes you need to come home to someone who still wants to be with you after you bitch about how a costar got jizz in your eye when he came on your face.

Every boyfriend except Jay, that is. He was the only one I ever really cared about. But he'd been disappointing in a different way. Like the car enthusiast he was, he couldn't resist trading in his old ride for a shiny new one.

"You remember those *Virgin High* videos I told you about?" Krystal asked Terry.

"What, with the chick on the balance beam?"

"Parallel bars," I said.

"This is her!"

"No shit," Terry said. He put his arm around Krystal's shoulders and crushed her to him. "I bet you could fuck on the balance beam no problem, right, baby? Maybe you should do a remake."

I kept the smile on my face, but inside I cringed. There's a superstition in movies, in all entertainment probably, that once an idea is put out there, even as a joke, it will inevitably become a reality, as if somebody could pluck it right out of the air. If a remake of *Virgin High* happened with some new starlet in my signature role, I would personally hunt Terry down and kill him for bringing it up. Not that I'm a superstitious woman, but *Virgin High* was all the cred I had left.

"You still got that marker in your bag, hon?" Krystal asked. Terry swung the knapsack off his shoulder, rummaged through it and pulled out a black Sharpie. She snatched it out of his hand and put it in mine. "Do you mind?"

"No, sure, do you have something for me to sign?"

I expected her to produce a cocktail napkin or even one of her father's old video boxes, but instead she lifted her t-shirt up to her neck with both hands. "To Krystal," she said, "with a K."

Her breasts were enormous, way out of proportion with her tiny body. I was afraid the Sharpie might accidentally pop her implant when I pressed it to her left breast, but the opposite happened. As the felt tip of the marker squeaked over the skin just above her stretched nipple, it didn't even indent the flesh. I've signed a lot of tits in my time, but I'd never seen anything like that. It was like writing on a bowling ball. She should sue her plastic surgeon.

"Get the camera," she told Terry. He nodded and pulled out a sleek, silver digital number. "Can I get a shot of this?" she asked me.

"Sure," I said, "but I finished signing my name."

"Pretend you're still writing."

I held my hand over her breast, keeping the Sharpie's tip just above my signature. My arm began shaking with fatigue. As I watched my wrist tremble, I wondered what had happened to me. Time was, I could maintain a split on the parallel bars for fifteen minutes without so much as breaking a sweat, but now I was shaking like an old junkie just from holding a pen above some girl's tit while her mongoloid idiot boyfriend tried to figure out how to press a fucking button.

Finally, the flash went off. Krystal thanked me, and she and Terry wandered over to the coke table. She kept her shirt up to show off my signature. I needed to get away for a minute, so I went out into the back yard. No stars came through the smoggy night sky, and the moon was just a bright smear on the clouds. Bruce had set up tiki torches on the lawn, but that was more for effect than anything else, since the muggy night was keeping everyone inside with the air conditioning. I was alone in the orange glow of the flames.

I reached into my bag, fumbled for my pack of Newports, and lit up. My hand was still trembling. After being accosted by Little Miss Rock-Hard Abs, I felt old as dust and about as sexy. Maybe there was no place for me in the industry anymore. Part of me wanted to walk away and leave it all behind, forget Bruce's new movie, forget all hope of a comeback. How could I compete with the Krystal Lynns of the world?

But porn was all I knew and, frankly, all I wanted to know. The job only asked you to fuck some broad-shouldered hunk you'd probably want to fuck anyway, and by the end of the day you had enough money to make two months' rent. Everyone always said I was too smart for this business, but what else was I qualified to do? Waitress? Run daycare? *Hey, kids, did I ever tell you about the time Ron Jeremy shot his load on my tits and couldn't stop giggling?*

More than that, I didn't want to be just some *grande dame* with a Lifetime Achievement Award. I wanted to be the fantasy of pubescent boys everywhere, I wanted guys on their commutes to think of me and have no choice but to pull their cars over and jerk off. I wanted to be wanted again. Dubbing hardcore anime wasn't going to make that happen. Being back in front of the camera would.

I stamped out my cigarette and started toward the sliding glass door that led to the kitchen. But before I reached it, I caught shapes moving in the darkness of the yard, and I stopped. A couple I hadn't noticed before stood just beyond the glow of the tiki torches and the light spilling out from the house. The man was tall, slender, and stood as straight as a board. He wore a finely pressed suit and a tieless dress shirt, with one arm around the shoulders of the petite woman in a dark, slinky dress next to him. They were both looking at me. I felt uncomfortable, strangely embarrassed by their attention. Normally I want people's eyes on me—nobody gets into adult films because they're shy—but this was different. They were staring at me so *intensely*, like they were trying to see the bones beneath my skin. I hurried inside. I wanted to find Bruce, get the script from him, and pour as much Cristal down my throat as I could before going home to my empty little apartment with its reminders of Jay everywhere.

Rounding the corner from the kitchen to the living room, I found him. Bruce was leaning against the wall with a glass of white wine in one hand, some rolled up papers in the other. He was surrounded by a gaggle of starlets who laughed at everything he said and touched his arms and chest every chance they got. Bruce was never a handsome man, not even back when he didn't have to dye the gray out of his hair. He's got one of those noses that looks like it's been broken a few too many times, and a bushy mustache that looks like a fat caterpillar died on his lip. Still, money is money and power is power, and these girls could smell both on him. They would do anything for him, and he knew it.

When he saw me, he shouted over their heads, "Amber!" He waved me over. The girls reluctantly parted to let me through. A few of them looked me up and down with one of those *Who's this bitch?* expressions that comes with being cock-blocked. Bruce handed me the papers. "Here's the script," he said. "We start shooting tomorrow night."

As with most scripts for adult films, it was really just an outline. The movie would probably run an hour, but the script was only six pages long. I sat down on one of the Italian leather chairs in the living room, blocked out the laughter and clinking glasses, and read it. It was called *The Big Cumback*, about three slutty female gangsters, Sabrina, Katie, and Jess, who escape from jail and fuck their way to the top of the male-dominated criminal underground. I had to flip through it three times before the part Bruce had in mind for me even registered.

I jumped out of the chair and stormed all over the house looking for him. No one knew where he was. That meant he was in the bedroom with someone and didn't want to be disturbed. I didn't care, I threw open the bedroom door and marched right in. Bruce was sitting naked on the king-sized bed, his back against the cushioned headboard. Some starlet's head was between his legs, a cloud of blonde hair bobbing over his hairy gut like a poodle dancing for scraps. I couldn't see her face, just her bare ass in the air and, beneath it, the snake eye slit of her shaved pussy.

A momentary pang of jealousy hit me—I used to be the one he took to the bedroom at parties—but I shrugged it off and shook the script in the air. "What the fuck, Bruce?"

He didn't flinch or yell or even tell the girl to stop. He only sighed and played with her hair when he said, "What's the matter now?" His unfazed reaction only infuriated me further.

"I'm playing Sabrina's *mother*?" I shouted.

Bruce's cock slid out of the girl's mouth with a wet pop, and she glanced at me over her shoulder. It was Krystal Lynn. Why wasn't I surprised?

"Oh my God," Krystal said, *"you're* playing my mother? How awesome is that? We're going to be in a movie together!"

I glared at Bruce. "She's Sabrina?"

Bruce put a hand on Krystal's head and pushed her face down again. "Did I say you could stop?" Then he turned to me. "Relax, babe, it's a part, isn't it? You'll be on camera again like you wanted."

"I don't even have a goddamn sex scene, Bruce. I just come out of a shower and walk in on her and a guy—"

"It's not sex, but you'll still be naked. Everyone will see your tits, everyone will see your bush, I promise you. That gets you back in the public eye. And it's a funny scene, too. You do comedy well, I've seen it."

I shook the script at him again. "This is bullshit and you know it. I can do more than this. You *owe* me, Bruce. I put *Virgin High* on the fucking map, I made you who you are today."

He sat up, and Krystal made a little gagging sound as she readjusted. "I'm the one sticking his neck out even putting you in the movie at all! The real bullshit here is thinking our audience wants to watch a forty-year-old woman fuck. Have you seen the new movies Marilyn Chambers is doing? They're shit and they do shit business, but even she knows she's better off hosting them than having any sex scenes."

"I'm not Marilyn Chambers, I'm Amber fucking Fox! Do you know how much fan mail I still get?" It was a lie, I didn't get much at all, maybe a letter every couple of months, but I was hoping Bruce didn't know that.

"The audience has moved on, Amber. Your DVD reissues

aren't even selling. They don't care about you, they want new girls like Krystal here. She's going to be huge. Bigger than Chasey Lain, bigger than Tera Patrick, she's the next Jenna Jameson, and I'm not going to fuck up her big break by putting *anything* in the movie the fans don't want to see."

"The next Jenna?" Krystal asked. "You really think so?"

"You know it, babe." He guided her head down again.

"Bruce," I said, "just give me a chance—"

"Enough, Amber. Get this straight. Most of our customer base is in their teens and twenties. It's not that they don't remember you, they've never *heard* of you. You might as well be their mother, and no one wants to watch their mother fuck. The script is what it is, there won't be any changes. If you don't like it, find someone else to put you in a movie. Oh, that's right, I forgot. No one else will."

I turned on my heel and stomped toward the door.

"One more thing," Bruce called after me. I half-expected him to say, *I've decided to remake* Virgin High *and give Krystal your role—I plucked the idea right out of the air,* but instead he motioned toward my crotch and said, "Be sure to trim your pussy before we start shooting. Or better yet, shave the whole thing clean. This isn't the Eighties anymore, no one wants to see a jungle down there."

I slammed the bedroom door behind me. I could hear the party raging, laughter and popping champagne corks and a loud, arrogant voice somewhere announcing, "I own Sunset Auto Parts," but I didn't want to deal with the crowd. I ducked into the bathroom, locked the door, and ran the faucet into the shell-shaped marble sink. I splashed bracing cold water on my face, then scrutinized myself in the mirror. I looked myself up and down, turned to the side to check my stomach, turned around to check my ass. I'd taken care of myself over the years. I hadn't turned into a cow like Marilyn Chambers, or gone craggy and gray like Georgina Spelvin. I looked *good*. So what the fuck was Bruce's problem?

"Keep your eye on the goal," I muttered to my reflection. I was going to be in front of the camera again. Bruce might have cast me thinking it was a kitschy cameo, but for me it was a whole lot more. It was the start of my comeback. I wouldn't let it be anything less. I'd do whatever it took to stand out, to be noticed in this role so people would say, *Holy shit, Amber Fox is back? I can't wait to see that!*

But first I had to get the hell out of this party. If I had to look at Bruce or Krystal Lynn one more time tonight, I'd go ballistic. I opened the bathroom door, stepped out into the hall—

And nearly bumped into the couple I'd seen outside. They were standing in the middle of the hallway, blocking my path. In the light, I could better see the olive complexion of their skin, the pitch blackness of their hair.

"You are Amber?" the man said. He had a slight accent I couldn't place.

"The one and only." I was nervous because they were staring at me with the same intensity as before, so the old joke came out of my mouth automatically. I tried to move past them, but they wouldn't get out of my way.

"Allow me to introduce myself," he said. "I am Ashraf Hammad, and this is my wife Raha." The woman nodded, her dark eyes glistening, but didn't say a word. "We enjoy your movies."

"That's great," I said. I felt bad for blowing off fans, but I was so desperate to get out of that house I'd stampede over them if I had to. "Excuse me—"

Raha raised one small tan hand, her palm an inch from my face. I froze, thinking the crazy bitch was going to slap me, but then something happened. The space between her hand and my skin suddenly felt like it was inhabited by a thousand tongues, a thousand caressing lips. She moved her hand over my face and down my neck.

"No, I..." But I couldn't finish protesting. Instead, I closed my eyes and gave in to the sensation. I couldn't help myself.

"We were hoping to find you here tonight," Ashraf said softly. "You are more experienced than the others. You have what we need."

Raha moved her hand over my breasts, and though she never actually touched me, the sensation coaxed a loud moan from my throat. I leaned back against the wall and put my hands in my hair. Raha moved her hand lower.

"She likes you," Ashraf told me. "You should be honored."

"I…really have to go," I managed to say.

Raha cupped her hand at my groin. I gasped as those thousand invisible tongues stroked between my legs. I felt myself getting wet.

"No," I said, pushing her away. There was something unnatural about this. Who were these people? How was she doing that with her hand?

"Why do you resist?" Ashraf asked. He sounded genuinely confused.

"I don't understand what's happening to me," I said, trying to catch my breath. I still had to lean against the wall for support.

"You do not need to understand," he said. He started unbuttoning his dress shirt. "All you need to know is that you have been chosen." He pulled the shirt open, and there on his chest, hanging from a thin chain around his neck, was a gold medallion. At first I thought it was an eye like the kind you see in Egyptian hieroglyphics, but as I looked closer I saw it was made up of smaller geometric shapes, triangles and circles. The center seemed to be moving, swirling, as if an entire galaxy of stars were hidden inside it.

"Your necklace," I said. I felt warm, feverish, dizzy. "Moving…"

"It is not the necklace that moves," he said. "It is the Eye."

Raha smiled. It was the most beautiful smile I'd ever seen. The desire to kiss her came over me without warning. I wanted to see what was under that dress, run my hands through her thick black hair, my lips over her bare skin, kiss every inch of her. And when I looked at Ashraf, I wanted more than anything to please him. I would do whatever he wanted. The need for them both burned inside me like an unquenchable fire.

I went with them to their car. I let Raha run her hands all over my body in the back seat while Ashraf drove. I didn't care where we were going. I never wanted the ride to end. When it did, we were in an enormous house in the Hollywood Hills. I didn't remember leaving the car or walking inside, I simply found myself lying on a luxurious bed in the middle of a room with big stone walls. My dress and underwear were on the floor, but I had no memory of taking them off. Raha appeared above me, nude, straddling me on her hands and knees. Her midnight hair cascaded around my head. When I reached up for her, my hands cupped soft, pointed breasts with hard, dark nipples.

Ashraf walked around the bed, still fully clothed. He looked at the stone walls and the symbols etched into them. I didn't recognize any of the carvings, except the same eye he had on his medallion was on each wall.

Raha bent down and kissed my breasts, suckling the nipples until they stood almost painfully erect. I arched my back in ecstasy and wrapped my legs around her. I was so wet I thought a flood would pour out of me.

Ashraf's voice floated through the room, echoing off the stone. "It is said that in the time of the Ancients, Ra, the greatest of all the gods, grew disgusted at man's disregard for his laws. In his anger, he created Sekhmet, the Eye of Ra, the goddess of destruction, a bare-breasted woman with the head of a lioness, and unleashed her upon man to reap vengeance."

Raha moved lower, kissing my belly. I squirmed and moaned on the bed. The inferno raging between my legs could only be extinguished by her tongue.

"The Nile turned crimson from all the blood she shed. When Ra saw the horror he had created, he regretted his actions. He laid a trap for her, hundreds of barrels of beer stained red with pomegranate juice to resemble the blood she enjoyed drinking."

Raha ran her tongue lightly over my pussy, from bottom to top. I shivered and arched my back again. It wouldn't take much more to make me come. I could feel it building already, dancing on the cusp of onset.

Ashraf appeared behind Raha. He removed his shirt and let it drop to the floor. I couldn't take my eyes off the medallion hanging over his chest.

"Ra's plan worked," he continued, undoing his belt. "Sekhmet grew drunk and fell asleep."

I ran my fingers through Raha's thick hair. "Oh God, don't stop."

Ashraf bent to remove his shoes. I watched the well-defined

muscles move under the skin of his torso. I wanted him inside me so badly. Raha's lips on my clit made me gasp.

"While she slept, Ra made it so Sekhmet forgot who she was and the destruction she spread across the Kingdom." Ashraf hooked his thumbs inside his pants and pushed them down. He wasn't wearing anything underneath. "Ra changed her name to Hathor so she would never have to remember her deeds. Her nature was changed also, to the sweetness of love and the strength of desire." He stepped toward the bed, his heavy cock growing bigger, stiffer, as he approached. "And henceforth Hathor laid low men and women only with the great power of love."

I looked at Raha between my legs again, but my vision blurred and for a moment I didn't see her, only what looked like the shaggy pyramid ears and tawny pelt of a lioness, black-and-yellow eyes hovering over my pubic hair like twin moons. I closed my eyes, letting the feel of her tongue take me to the very edge of climax.

And then she stopped.

Panting for breath, I opened my eyes again. Raha crawled up the bed to lay down beside me. She kissed me, her mouth flavored with the vinegar tang of my pussy, and her fingertips played lightly over my nipples.

"That is the story they tell," Ashraf said. He grabbed my ankles and pulled me down until my ass was at the bottom edge of the bed. Raha turned, kissing me upside-down. "But it is not the whole story." He pushed my legs up and apart. "How is it, do you think, that Ra *really* tamed a woman as wild as Sekhmet?"

I started coming the moment he slid his cock inside me, wave after crashing wave of intense orgasms. I thrashed on the bed, made noises I'd never made before, as he slowly pulled out, almost to the point of exit, then rammed it back in. Every time he did, I shuddered with a new climax.

"What incentive do you think Ra promised her to keep the goddess of desire from turning back into the goddess of destruction?" he asked.

Raha crawled on top of me, still upside-down, spreading her

thighs over my face. Between Ashraf's slow and steady thrusts and Raha's tongue on my clit again, I came so hard I thought I might pass out. Little white dots exploded behind my eyelids. I wrapped my hands around the smooth skin of her ass and eagerly pulled her cunt down to my mouth. She didn't make a sound, only ground her hips above my head and continued licking me.

"It was Isis and Osiris who valued virgins, not Hathor. Hathor had little patience for teaching them the way of pleasure. She treasured experience above all else."

Raha shuddered hard, pushing her cunt right up against my face as she came. Now, finally, a sound escaped her throat as the orgasm steamrolled through her, a low, guttural cry that echoed off the stone walls like a roar. Hearing her come made me so hot I thought my skin would burst into flames.

"Ra promised her lovers of exceptional experience. He fashioned the Eye of Hathor, a powerful symbol that awakens in all who see it an irresistible desire, in order to procure lovers for her."

Raha lifted one leg and swung herself off of me. Ashraf pulled out, his cock dripping wet. I moaned in disappointment, but Raha silenced me with a deep kiss, our tongues dancing around each other like frisky cubs. Ashraf took hold of each of my legs and pushed them up until my knees were against my chest. Then, effortlessly, he thrust his cock into my ass.

I've done a lot in my career, girl-on-girl, two guys at once, bukkake trains, you name it, but the one thing I *never* did was anal. It'd always been off limits, even in my private life. But I was so hot, so willing to do anything he wanted, that I didn't care. It didn't hurt like I thought it would, either. His cock slid right in on the natural lubricant from my sopping pussy. It was the most incredible feeling. Raha kept kissing me, working my clit with her finger until I was on the brink of orgasm again. Then she stuck her finger inside me, and I came harder than I had all night.

Ashraf's breath caught in his throat. He tilted his head back, his mouth hanging open. I felt his cock stiffen in my ass, then pull out. He climbed onto the bed, holding his prick in one hand, and positioned himself on his knees above Raha and me. The first hot spurt of semen hit my face, cooling immediately as it rolled down my chin. Raha opened her mouth to receive the second, and I did the same. A few moments later, his cock drooped, spent, and our lips, chins and cheeks were coated in a thick white goo. Raha kissed me once more, her mouth slippery and salty.

I looked at Ashraf above me, the golden Eye of Hathor glittering on his heaving, sweaty chest. I stretched out on the bed, a satisfied hum buzzing through my body. I'd almost forgotten what it's like to be so wanted.

My eyelids drooped as the afterglow pulled me toward sleep. I saw Ashraf bend over me, the medallion flashing, then there was only a warm darkness. And yet, I could still see the medallion burning brightly in my mind, in perfect detail. I felt arms around me, as if I was being carried, and when I opened my eyes we were in the car again. My clothes had reappeared on my body. I closed my eyes, wanting to sink back into the comfortable blackness, and saw the medallion once more behind my eyelids.

"The Eye," I managed to say, little more than a whisper. "It's in my head…"

"Our gift to you, in thanks," Ashraf 's voice replied. "Any who gaze upon it will be yours. Choose wisely."

I opened my eyes once more and saw Raha sitting next to me. I put my hand to her cheek. "Will I see you again?"

She shook her head, and from the front seat, Ashraf said, "We will not meet again, nor will we be here if you come looking for us. It is the way."

I nodded sadly, closing my eyes only for a moment. When I opened them again I was slumped in the driver's seat of my car on the empty street outside Bruce's house. The sun was coming up, tinting everything gray. I shook the cobwebs out of my head and drove home. The Eye of Hathor burned in my mind the whole way there. It was there when I collapsed onto my bed, and when I woke up a few hours later with Bruce's words circling my brain like song lyrics that get stuck in your head: *Everyone will see your tits, everyone will see your bush, I promise you.*

If he wanted me to trim my pubes before the shoot, there was only one man in all of L.A. for the job. He called himself the Gardener, and everyone who was anyone used him when it was grooming time. After calling to make an appointment, I drove to his home office in Orange County.

"Amber!" he exclaimed, greeting me at the door in an orange Polo shirt that almost matched the color of his Irish hair. "How long has it been?"

"Too long," I said, hugging him. He invited me into his living room, where big glossy photos of his work adorned the walls, women's nude crotches with all manner of shaved pubic hair: the standard landing strip, a Valentine's heart, a jack o'lantern, a Christmas tree, a lightning bolt, even the Gucci symbol. When I told him what I wanted and asked if he could do it, he spread his hands and said, "Hey, I'm the Gardener, aren't I?"

He brought me into the brightly lit, white-walled room in back, where there were two tables of shaving equipment and, in the center, a large barber-style chair tilted back with two silver stirrups protruding from the seat. I dropped my skirt, my panties, and sat, nude from the waist down, on the chair. I stuck my heels in the stirrups and rolled my blouse up a bit.

The Gardener knelt down on the floor between my legs, first trimming the hair with electric clippers, then dipping his fingertips in a jar of petroleum jelly and gently smearing a thin layer over the fine fuzz in slow circles. Finally, he picking up his trusty straightedge. I painstakingly guided him through the process, describing everything down to the minutest detail. Two hours in, my cell phone rang. I fished it out of my purse and looked at the caller ID. It was Bruce.

"So," he said, "are you all set for tonight?"

"You bet. I'm at the Gardener's now, getting a shave just like you said." I felt the blade clear away the last of the extra hair. He was finished.

"How's it look?" Bruce asked.

"Hold on, I'll find out. How's it look?" I asked the Gardener. He didn't answer. He stared at my crotch, transfixed. Under his belt buckle, I could see his cock stiffening, straining against his fly. "I'd say it looks pretty damn good," I said into the phone.

"Great," Bruce said. "The camera is going to love you, babe."

The Gardener couldn't control himself anymore. He leaned forward, put his hands on my thighs, and started eating me out, his tongue disappearing beneath the Eye of Hathor shaved into my pubic hair.

"Bruce," I said, "once this movie comes out, *everyone* is going to love me."

GO

"Go" was originally supposed to appear in an animals-gone-wild anthology called Tooth & Claw, Vol. 2, but alas, the Tooth & Claw series never made it past volume one. As a result, it became an unintended original in Walk In Shadows, and garnered the most fan mail of any story I've written. Everyone seemed to love it, and equally, everyone hated the ending. Actually, hate doesn't seem like a strong enough word for how people felt about the way I leave this story. But I love this story to pieces, and I love anyone who loves it as much as I do.

1.

From the instruction and usage manual for the GS-431 Surveillance System at Kiernan Clinical Research:
Blood looks black on the video monitors.

2.

The message Britt left on Jeff's answering machine last night was gnawing at him. His ex-wife wasn't sure if she would be able to drop their son off at Kiernan's day care in the morning. "I know tomorrow's Friday and it's your weekend with Chris," Britt said. "I'm really sorry about this, but my friend Claire might need me to go with her to the doctor in the morning because she's getting her test results, and I don't know yet if I'm going to have time to drop him off first. Chris is okay with waiting until Saturday to see you, and I hope you'll be okay with this, too. But since Claire doesn't know all the details yet, this is just sort of a heads-up. I'll let you know either way."

Of course, she never called back. Jeff called her first thing in the morning but there was no answer.

It gnawed at him the whole drive to work.

He and Britt had a civil relationship whenever it came to Chris: Chris's health, Chris's friends, Chris's behavior, Chris's eye troubles—his left eye was weaker than his right, so for the last few weeks he'd been wearing a patch over the healthier eye to strengthen the other. He looked like a little pirate to Jeff, but the poor five-year-old was so embarrassed by it he felt nervous every time he left the house. Chris was the best thing to come out of Jeff and Britt's seven-year marriage, and they both knew it.

But this was enormously inconsiderate, considering he only got to see Chris on Fridays, Saturdays and Sundays. She got the rest of the week. It was just plain selfish of her, holding onto Chris an extra day.

Jeff took a deep breath, let it out slowly.

It wasn't really Britt bothering him. It was what she said: *Chris is okay with waiting until Saturday to see you.* Why would Chris be okay with waiting when he only spent a few days a week with Jeff? Wasn't he a fun dad? Didn't he always have ice cream and cookies waiting? Didn't he always rent fun movies for them to watch; take Chris to places like the zoo and the children's museum?

Wasn't he a good dad?

Jeff pulled into the research center's parking lot and slammed the car door closed.

The usual crowd of protesters waited by the entrance to the single-story research center, hoisting signs denouncing the cruelty of animal testing, chanting, shouting. The morning sun cast their shadows against the corrugated metal of the building's retractable firewalls.

Jeff saw this group every day, and though he didn't know their names he'd invented a few. There was Unwashed Mountain Man, whose long hair and beard were a tangled mess; Heidi, with her long blonde braids and razor-thin lips; Ganja Sam, with eyes redder than a stop sign and a wool cap on his head no matter what the weather; Pippi Longstocking, with her dark red hair, fishnets and Doc Martens; Shaggy and Velma, an inseparable couple, he with the hairy chin, she with the thick glasses; and Hippy Chick, who wore translucent white peasant shirts with no bra beneath. She was Jeff's favorite, of course, and he always made sure to nod good morning to her as he walked past, even while she spat at him and called him a murderer. It would do no good to explain that he was just a security guard, not one of the scientists.

Up ahead, past the jumble of placards and shouting heads, Jeff caught a flash of straight, strawberry blonde hair swaying briskly as someone walked toward the entrance. Britt? Jeff weaved his way through the crowd of protesters, trying not to lose sight of her.

Unwashed Mountain Man got in his face. "Murderer!" he yelled. "Murderer!" His breath reeked of tuna fish and pot.

Jeff tried to see past him, but the woman who might be Britt was gone.

"Move," Jeff said, grabbing the protester's shoulders and shifting him aside.

"Did you see that?" Unwashed Mountain Man hollered to the crowd. "He attacked me!"

Darren, one of Jeff's fellow security guards, appeared out of the crowd. Darren was stuck with door duty for the second day in a row; he must've really done something to piss off the chief of security.

"He manhandled me!" Unwashed Mountain Man hollered again.

"Fuck off," Darren said. He motioned to Jeff. "Come on, Shaffer. Get your ass inside already."

Jeff followed him to the door. "Did you see Britt come through here with my kid?"

Darren shrugged. "I was too busy saving you from a Granola pelting."

"Let me know if you see them, all right?"

Inside, instead of walking to the security locker room, Jeff made for the day care center in the far wing of the building. It always felt different there, more inviting, more comfortable; the pale yellow cinderblock walls were decorated with children's drawings of houses and families and bright yellow suns with straight lines coming out of them, M-shaped birds and puffy clouds and stick figure dogs. The antiseptic air fresheners did their best to mask the thick smell of monkey hair, dirt and feces emanating from the lab on the other side of the building. Jeff barely noticed it anymore.

Leann Hopkins ran day care alone on Fridays. She was a pretty, dark-haired woman in her mid-twenties who studied Child Development in college and was getting her grad in Psychology. Leann had a killer body, and she swore like a sailor when she wasn't around the kids.

Once, Jeff was outside in the parking lot with her, sharing a cigarette break at the end of the day, when he heard her say "motherfucker" for the first time, and he immediately wanted to screw her. He pictured it often, always the same way: the parking lot, Leann against the hood of a red sports car, Jeff on top of her, her arms tightening around his back—*Oh God, you're amazing, you're an animal!*

Classic mid-life crisis fantasy, right down to the sports car. Except at thirty-seven Jeff didn't feel nearly mid-life yet. Divorced from Britt, he felt as if his life were just starting.

He saw Leann up ahead, ushering a little girl into the room. Leann wore a brown sweater top and dark jeans, her hair pulled back in a small ponytail. She stepped into the room, reaching back to close the door behind her.

Jeff quickened his pace, about to call out to her when a hand wrapped around his elbow, stopping him.

It was Gary, already suited up in his security uniform. He looked anxious.

"Jeff, we need you," he said. "Something happened." He led Jeff back in the other direction.

"What is it?"

"The six A.M. shot," Gary said. He sounded out of breath. "I wasn't here yet, it wasn't my shift. Somehow one of them got out of its cage. Taylor, I think. Almost bit Dr. Bradley's hand clean off."

3.

From a letter written by Dr. Linda Bradley to her boyfriend in England:

Technically, they're called papio ursinus, also known as the chacma, the largest of the baboon family. An adult male weighs in at ninety pounds. They can be very aggressive, with strong jaws, even stronger limbs and an incredible sense of smell. The chacma will eat anything with the bad luck to be in front of it at suppertime, including small mammals, even other monkeys. The adult males are so vicious that even leopards, their principal enemy, tend to avoid them.

Put one of these blokes in a cage and it won't be pleased.

Pump it full of experimental vaccine KC-488—side effects so far: dry mouth, diarrhea (guess who gets to clean up that mess?), restlessness, increased appetite—and you've really pissed it off.

Now multiply that pissed-off baboon by a dozen and you've got Kiernan Clinical Research, my new employer in the States. Wish me luck. I'm going to need it.

4.

Dan Montgomery, the chief of security, waited for them in the locker room. "Dr. Bradley's all right," he said. "They took her to the hospital earlier. I don't know when she'll be back, though."

Jeff and Gary looked at each other.

Dan nodded to Jeff. "Better get suited up and into the Box, Shaffer. It's going to be that kind of day."

Jeff went to his locker. "What about Taylor?"

"Taylor's back in his cage." Dan shook his head. "Fucking monkeys. It was only a matter of time."

"You guys didn't happen to see my kid this morning, did you?"

They both said no. "Too much going on," Dan said.

Jeff pulled his tan security uniform over his undershirt.

"How'd Taylor get out in the first place?"

Dan shrugged. "No one knows yet. Dr. Bradley said his cage was already unlocked when she started her injection rounds this morning. When she got to him, he jumped her."

Jeff checked his handgun before holstering it: a SIG Arms P245 Compact with a short black grip and a blue barrel less than four inches long, built more for stopping than killing, though it was lethal at close range.

"Negligence," Gary said. "They'll blame security for this, no doubt."

"Or maybe," Jeff said, "Taylor opened it himself."

5.

Another letter from Dr. Linda Bradley to her boyfriend in England:

KC-488 is supposed to vaccinate against diseases like Creutzfeldt-Jakob, foot and mouth, and mad cow—enjoying those burgers in Coventry, darling?—but it's too soon to tell if we've got something good on our hands. The placebo prions we injected into the baboons may not be close enough to actual Transmissible Spongiform Encephalopathy, especially the bovine version, to give us good results. Aren't you glad you asked?

Plus, it's affecting their appetites. They can't seem to eat enough. We already have feedings scheduled every hour, and sometimes I think half our budget goes to food alone.

You asked about the baboons' names. Well, someone must've thought it would be funny to name them after Planet of the Apes, so we've got Taylor, Cornelius, Zaius, Galen, Caesar, etc. Someone ought to tell these esteemed scientists that baboons are not apes but monkeys, and thus the joke doesn't really work.

They're all male chacmas, but Taylor is the only one with blue skin on his face, and he's definitely a dominant, an alpha monkey. I know this is going to sound weird, but I don't like Taylor at all. He looks at me funny every time I walk past him, and he especially hates the injections. He grunts at me all the time, a sort of two-phase "uh-uh." I think he's threatening me. Maybe he blames me for the shots, for being locked up in a lab, whatever.

This part's even stranger, but I swear I saw him wave to me once. It wasn't a friendly sort of "hello there" wave, it was something else. Almost as if he were showing me something about his hand. He wiggled his fingers in a strange way. I can't really explain it.

6.

Box duty was the best any security guard at Kiernan could hope for. Where door duty meant dealing with the protesters all day, and floor duty meant standing for the whole eight-hour shift, the surveillance room—affectionately known as the Box—was comparative luxury.

A ten-by-ten room adjacent to the lab, it was the only on-duty site where a guard was allowed to sit. The far wall, across from the door, was one huge bank of video monitors, the GS-431 Surveillance System, each linked to a camera trained on a specific location: hallways, cafeteria, secure areas, but mostly the lab itself. Each of the twelve baboons had a camera fixed on its cage. More cameras in the corners of the room, and even a camera pointed directly outside the Box itself.

The tinted light from the black-and-white monitors played across Jeff's face as he sat back and watched.

The scientists roamed the floor of the lab outside, clipboards in hand, speaking into small micro-cassette recorders, looking at charts, poking, prodding, talking amongst themselves. Then it was feeding time again—every hour on the hour or the baboons got restless—and the baboons snatched fruit from the scientists' hands, tearing into the apples, pears, mangoes and bananas with their huge canines. Their long, dog-like muzzles were wet with juice, gnashing and spitting.

Jeff only knew a few of the scientists by name. One of them, Dr. Alonso, had a crush on him, or so the other guards teased. She was always telling him to call her Veronica; always smiling at him and saying hello. She was a good-looking woman, with a long ponytail of straight black hair and a curvy body, and though Jeff certainly enjoyed the attention, she wasn't the one on the sports car in his fantasies.

A quick glance at the monitors showed Veronica talking to Dr. DeFranco, with his trademark bow tie peeking out between the lapels of his lab coat. The unexpected twinge of jealousy surprised Jeff.

Another monitor caught his eye. One of the baboons stared up from behind the bars of its cage, looking directly into the camera. The nameplate on the cage read TAYLOR.

The baboon didn't look away. Its gaze was fixed on the camera, eyebrows raised, scalp tightened, ears back, stretching the skin of its face, making its eyes look bigger.

Something in those eyes made Jeff uncomfortable.

He took a deep breath and forced himself to look away.

He wished one of the cameras looked in on day care, but it wasn't allowed. Something about privacy laws. There was a camera right outside day care, though, and with luck maybe someone would open the door and he'd get a peek inside.

He sighed, getting angry again. This was ridiculous, locked away by himself in the Box, playing eyes and ears for the security team, not even knowing if his son were here or not.

What are you going to do now, sport?

7.

Were there ever two brothers as inseparable as Jeff and Stephen Shaffer?

Every available moment was spent together in constant competition: who could run the fastest, swim the farthest, eat the most pizza; and later, who would have the most dates in a month, who could do more sit-ups, whose facial hair grew in darker.

Jeff felt like he spent forever trying to catch up to his big brother. Nothing influenced the course of his life more. When Stephen died just over a year ago, when the cancer found his brain and switched it off like a desk lamp, Jeff wept, screamed, punched a hole in the wall, kicked over the TV stand and scared Britt so much she ran, without looking back, right into the arms of another man.

What are you going to do now, sport?

They were Stephen's words, and he heard them often these days. He carried Stephen's voice inside him like a compass, letting it guide him, inspire him, keep him going no matter what. In a way, it was still the same brotherly competition: if Stephen could handle his illness with such courage and grace, Jeff could handle his divorce.

He remembered when Stephen was eleven, Jeff was nine, and the back yard seemed enormous, how Stephen would taunt him, holding the Frisbee behind his back, away from Jeff. Stephen would say, "What are you going to do now, sport?" as Jeff grew more eager, more frustrated in his attempt to snatch it away from him. Then Stephen would take the Frisbee and whip it hard across the yard. He'd shout, "Go!" and Jeff would take off after it.

All the while Marie, their babysitter, would shake her head and say, "If you little monkeys kill yourselves, I won't get paid, so you'd better take care and not run around like someone chopped your tails off."

Jeff loved how she called them little monkeys. She even taught them a song. She said it was from her village in Jamaica, an old song carried over from West Africa, but Jeff and Stephen didn't believe her. They knew the song was about them.

What do the monkey say?
What do the monkey say?
What do the monkey say?
Monkey say ah-ah.

8.

Jeff wasn't sure what made him look up at that particular monitor just then. Maybe it was a flash of movement; maybe it was the muffled drum of instinct inside him. He looked up and saw that same baboon, Taylor, doing something strange with his hands, as if he were motioning to the other baboons in the cages around him.

Taylor wiggled his fingers in a strange way.

Jeff glanced at the other monitors in quick succession.

Eleven other baboons sat quietly in their cages, captivated, looking at something.

Looking at Taylor.

Taylor motioned again.

What the hell are they doing? Jeff thought.

The lab staff was gathered at a counter at one end of the room, comparing notes, talking, oblivious. Bits of their conversation floated to the camera's microphone.

"...more feedings..."

"...the fruit doesn't seem to be enough anymore..."

"...it's making them more restless, look at how Dr. Bradley was attacked..."

Jeff watched as all twelve baboons wiggled their fingers like Taylor.

Taylor opened his mouth, showed his long teeth, and the other baboons started barking.

Taylor reached forward, through the bars of his cage, moving his fingers. The others did the same.

Jeff leaned toward the monitors. "What the fuck...?"

And all twelve cages swung open.

9.

From Dr. Linda Bradley's final letter before the incident:

Taylor still gives me the wonks, but I've noticed he's an excellent mimic. More than once I've caught him imitating—funny, I was about to write "aping"—my colleagues' faces. He's especially good at doing Dr. Henderson, puffing out his cheeks and extending his lower lip. Henderson was not amused.

Yesterday, I was opening Urko's cage for the 6 AM shot, and I saw Taylor watching me. He waved again, that strange thing he does with his fingers, and for a moment I could've sworn he wasn't looking at me but at the sliding deadbolts on the door of Urko's cage, as if he were trying to mimic the motions it took to open it.

You'll probably think I'm daft, but I'm going to talk to Upper Management about changing these locks, maybe to something heavier involving a key or combination.

10.

Too late.

Jeff's thumb practically broke the plastic shell of the alarm button on the control desk. Shrill sirens, flashing lights...

Too late.

By the time the scientists turned around, the baboons were out.

Chaos. Barking. Grunting. Cages knocked over. Papers, utensils, beakers, invaluable electron microscopes, delicate centrifuges, all thrown, tossed, swept aside.

One of the scientists screamed.

On one monitor, Jeff saw Dan Montgomery spin around, grab the radio off his shoulder and look up into the camera. "Shaffer, come in."

Jeff grabbed his radio. "Containment breach, main lab."

Dan turned around, motioned for the other guards, then looked up at the camera again. "How many?"

Jeff's hand faltered on the radio for a moment. "All of them."

Dan stared up at the camera, the muscles of his face slowly going slack. On the monitor, surrounded by all the other black-and-white video screens, he looked very small.

Then Dan turned, motioning off-camera again. "Move!"

Another monitor: a case of six tranquilizer rifles on a wall; a hand fitting a key into the lock; more hands, grabbing the rifles from their stations.

Jeff turned, looked at the rifle case on the Box wall. One rifle, holding one dart at a time, just like the ones outside. It wouldn't be enough.

Something banged against the metal door behind him, shaking it in its frame.

Jeff looked up at the monitors. A baboon squatted in front of the Box, then raised itself up on its thick, sturdy legs, extended its arms in front of it, and launched itself at the door again.

Heart pounding, Jeff's eyes moved frantically from one monitor to the next, trying to take in all the images.

The scientists were huddled in one corner of the lab,

crouching low, trying to stay out of harm's way.

Taylor was on top of a long counter in the middle of the room, grunting as he knocked everything to the floor and tossed papers into the air.

The other baboons, their teeth bared, stalked the floor on hands and feet, their short tails arched behind them, rummaging through the mess and barking to each other. Jeff heard it all around him: coming loudly through the door and softly through the weak camera microphones hooked to the monitors. One baboon shoved some paper into its mouth, then spat it out again with an angry grunt.

Food, Jeff thought. *They're looking for food.*

In the hallway outside the lab, Dan Montgomery and all five guards on staff—even Darren from door duty—ran for the lab door, tranquilizer rifles in hand.

The final monitor showed Jeff a hallway on the other side of the building, empty and silent, papered with children's drawings.

"Oh, God..."

11.

From an internal memo, corporate headquarters to the security staff:

The management is proud to announce the addition of free day care for all employees at Kiernan Clinical Research, including the security staff.

Obviously, this exciting new benefit brings with it some additional and important security protocols. In the event of an emergency, the children and day care staff must be escorted out of the building by at least one security officer. Please be advised that all day care staff members have been informed to remain in the day care facility with the children until a security officer arrives to escort them.

12.

On the monitors, Jeff watched the door to the lab burst open. Dan entered first, the five other guards coming in behind him and spreading out on either side, tranquilizer rifles raised.

Taylor turned to face them, letting out a shrill bark of alarm. The other baboons stopped what they were doing and watched.

Silence. No one moved.

Dan aimed the rifle at Taylor.

Taylor remained still.

Dan pulled the trigger, and Taylor jumped back with shrill cry, a pixilated blur on the video screen.

Jeff held his breath, didn't even blink.

Taylor stood up slowly on his thick hind legs and presented one hand.

In that hand, he held the tranquilizer dart.

Dan lowered the rifle slowly, his eyes wide.

Taylor leapt off the table, and at the same time the other baboons sprang forward. The other guards took aim with their rifles while Dan tried to stuff another dart into his.

They didn't have time to fire any shots before the baboons mobbed them.

13.

Blood looks black on the video monitors.

14.

Jeff, stunned, could only watch on the monitors as it all happened.

The baboons sprang on the guards with ferocious speed, clubbing at them with their fists, jumping on them and pulling them down. The guards swung their rifles like baseball bats, trying to knock the baboons away but it was six against twelve.

Darren was the first to go down when a baboon leapt

onto his chest, knocking him to the floor. Hairy fists pounded Darren's face until a pool of black obscured his features. Then it opened its mouth and sank its teeth into Darren's neck, pulling away with a wet chunk of skin and gristle.

Darren, shaking and weak, pulled his handgun from the holster on his belt, put it under the baboon's stomach, and pulled the trigger. The blast knocked it off him, and it landed at Darren's feet.

Neither got back up.

Dr. DeFranco screamed, jumped up, started running. A baboon hurled itself out of the fray and onto DeFranco's back, bringing him down by the tall chrome refrigerator against the wall. It grabbed DeFranco's head and bashed him twice, hard, against the floor. The scientist stopped moving, and a pool of black spread out under him.

The baboon grabbed DeFranco's arm and bit deep, right through the cloth of his lab coat, tearing out a chunk of meat. It sat down, chewed, swallowed and went back for more.

The guards threw down their tranquilizer rifles, drew their handguns and started firing. Dan Montgomery shouted for the lab staff to get out.

The baboon feeding on DeFranco's body collapsed with a bullet in its back.

More screaming, more pixilated chaos. Jeff finally broke away from the video monitors and grabbed the phone.

15.

"Dan, come in," Jeff shouted into the radio. "The police are on their way with backup; we've got an ETA of ten minutes."

On the monitor, Jeff saw Dan grab the radio off his shoulder and look up at the camera. "Roger that."

"I'm coming out," Jeff said, reaching for his holster.

"Negative, Shaffer. Stay in the Box, maintain contact with backup, and keep me informed. We've got to secure the area and get these people out. Keep your eyes on the monitors. If a single baboon gets past us, I want to know about it."

"Dan," Jeff said, "my kid…"

Dan's face froze. "Christ, day care. All right, Shaffer, if your kid's here, I'll get him out."

A blur of movement obscured the monitor. A baboon slammed into Dan's chest, knocking him to the floor. The pistol skittered out of his hand.

"Dan!"

The baboon's teeth tore into Dan's cheek. Dan struggled to push it away, but it held fast with its feet, then grabbed Dan's head and twisted. Dan's body went limp.

A shot from somewhere off-camera, and the baboon's head blew apart.

Jeff dropped the radio, drew his gun and went to the door. He looked back at the monitors. All clear outside the Box. He put a hand on the doorknob, took a deep breath, and pulled it open.

16.

Directly across the lab, Jeff saw the doorway and the four remaining security officers. Darren's body lay on the floor, beaten and bloody. Jeff could just make out Dan Montgomery's blood-streaked shoes where he lay.

The noise took him by surprise. Everything sounded distant over the monitors, and now it was all much louder: the explosive gunshots, the shrieking of the baboons as they mobbed and fell back, the fearful screams of the trapped scientists.

And the smell, that familiar monkey smell, mixed with the bitter tang of the guns and the copper salt of blood.

Jeff was barely out the door someone called his name. One of the scientists got up from where she was hiding and ran toward him.

Dr. Alonso.

Veronica.

"No!" Jeff shouted.

The baboon came out of nowhere, leaping over a counter and knocking her to the floor. With one hand splayed over her face, holding her down, it tore her lab coat open, ripped her blouse apart, and bit into the soft flesh of her stomach just below her black bra. Veronica screamed; only once, but it was long and it ended wetly.

Jeff swallowed hard, trying to keep his stomach down, and took aim at the baboon.

He heard the second baboon before he saw it, but he didn't turn in time, didn't have a chance to pull the trigger. It leapt on him, knocking him back into the Box and onto the floor.

The baboon was far stronger than Jeff imagined, and its overpowering stench filled his nostrils. It straddled Jeff's torso with its thick legs, barking furiously, its fists swinging through the air and landing on his face. One tough-skinned knuckle caught him on the lip, and he tasted blood.

Jeff tried to maneuver his gun hand under the baboon, but every hit to his face made him bring up both arms defensively. The baboon wrapped its hands around Jeff's face, squeezing tight and holding him down, then lowered itself toward his neck. The baboon's hot breath struck his skin; the tip of one huge canine brushed against his throat.

Jeff pulled up his knees, getting his legs under the baboon, and kicked it off him. It soared backward through the air, colliding with the door and knocking it closed. The baboon hit the floor, immediately sprang to its feet and came at him again, galloping on all fours.

Jeff grabbed its neck as it leapt for him, holding the baboon at arm's length as it struggled to hit, kick and bite. Jeff aimed his pistol into its open mouth and pulled the trigger. The kickback reverberated through his arm, and a spatter of crimson splashed the door. The baboon jerked in his grasp, then went limp. He dropped the body to the floor and stood there shaking, staring at it.

Jeff took a deep breath, pulling himself together, and looked back at the surveillance monitors.

The baboon was still on top of Veronica's corpse, reaching into the cavity in her torso, pulling out wet black things and tearing them with its teeth.

The other baboons mobbed the scientists, leaping onto them, beating them down, trying to bite them.

The lab doorway was empty; the guards were gone. Jeff swallowed hard. Was he the last?

And where the hell were the police? With no monitor hooked to a camera outside the building, he had no idea what was happening out there.

Five bullets left in his gun. He had to get out there, had to protect the scientists, get everyone out.

His eyes searched the monitors again, and his breath caught in his throat.

Two baboons trotted on all fours, their tails arched behind them, down a black-and-white hallway papered with children's drawings.

"Chris!" Jeff ran for the door, holding his gun ready.

He put a hand on the blood-slick doorknob.

Shrieks both human and baboon came from the other side, and the sound of overturned metal trays, shattering glass, wet gurgles, the thump of collapsing bodies.

What are you going to do now, sport?

He turned the knob.

Go!

17.

A baboon ran right for him before the door was even fully open, something large and round in its hands, obscured by thick hairy fingers. Jeff raised the gun.

It hurled the object at him, and when Jeff saw what it was his gun hand froze.

A human head.

He jumped back and slammed the door closed again. The head bounced off the other side with a hollow thud.

He stepped back again, and tripped over the dead baboon on the floor, landing in a puddle of its blood. His head spun, primal instinct and rational thought fighting for control.

Protect, run, get to safety, get back to the cave, hide from the enemy, from the predators...

Jeff grabbed the control desk in front of the monitors and

pulled himself up onto his knees. He had to keep it together, had to do his job.

On the monitor, the two baboons stopped in front of day care, sniffing at the gap in the door's base. One raised itself on its hind legs and started banging at the door.

Jeff—*run!*—tried to pull himself—*move!*—all the way up onto his feet—*protect!*—his eyes wide, fixed on the monitor.

The baboon banged on the day care door again.

Got to keep it together, got to get out there...

His legs wouldn't move. His whole body was cold, unresponsive. His vision grayed around the edges.

Going into shock...

It looked like the knob on the day care door was turning, but it was so small on the monitor he couldn't be sure.

No. He couldn't even shout it; but in his mind he could piece the horror together.

Leann, locked away in day care with the kids, the alarm blaring, not knowing what was going on—

Don't. What came out of his mouth was, "Uhhhh."

Leann, waiting for a security guard to come and tell her what was happening, to take them to safety—

Don't open that door.

Leann, finally hearing what sounded like a knock at the door, breathing a sigh of relief, telling the kids not to be scared, that they were finally going to find out what was going on, that it was probably a false alarm—

The day care door opened. Leann stood there, an expectant look on her face. When she saw the two baboons she put a hand to her mouth and screamed.

One baboon grabbed the hem of her sweater top and pulled, yanking her to the floor. Then they were both on top of her, clubbing her with their balled fists. Leann turned onto her side, inching toward the still-open door and reaching for the doorknob.

The first baboon grabbed her sweater again, trying to pull her back. The sweater stretched and tore, the neckline warping all the way down until it touched her belt. Her body, pale white on the monitor, was already scratched and bleeding. The second baboon grabbed her hair, breaking it out of its ponytail, pulling her head back, but still she reached for the doorknob.

Her hand touched the knob as she let out a guttural scream, her fingers wrapping around it.

For just a moment, Jeff could see the children in the room, staring out the doorway in horror, screaming, crying. One of them, tiny and distant on the monitor, wore an eye patch.

Like a little pirate.

Chris!

Leann pulled the door closed before the baboons overpowered her.

18.

A loud thump came from just outside the Box. The monitor showed a baboon banging and pushing against the door.

On another monitor, the two baboons were launching themselves at the door to day care again. Jeff couldn't see Leann, and he was glad for that.

Other monitors, more mayhem: half the scientists were dead, partially eaten, and the others were barricaded between an overturned table and the wall. Five baboons were trying to get through the gaps at the top and sides, and every time one got too close the scientists would poke at it with shards of glass from broken beakers and test tubes. It was only a matter of time before they'd be overpowered.

And still no sign of any of the other guards. He had to believe he was the last one left.

How much longer would it take the police to arrive? He grabbed the phone. No dial tone. The wires must've been damaged.

He'd have to go it alone. Chris and the other children were his immediate priority. The day care door looked like it was about to give; one of the baboons' fists splintered the wood and nearly broke through.

But with one baboon stationed outside the Box, five more waiting in the lab and two outside day care, how the hell would he make it there alive?

He'd have to get the baboons out of the way. But how?

He looked down at the control desk, at the only button that could help.

FIRE DOORS—EMERGENCY ONLY.

If he opened the retractable fire doors in the lab, there was a chance the baboons would leave. But he also knew what it would mean to press that button. He'd be letting those ravenous, drug-crazed baboons loose on the outside. Did he have it in him to do that? Were the protesters still there? Who else would be in their line of attack? Passers-by? Mothers with their children in tow? Elderly people out for an afternoon stroll? And what about the street? Car accidents, pile-ups, more casualties?

His hand hovered over the button.

The baboon outside the Box slammed into the door again.

What are you going to do now, sport?

The day care door cracked down the middle.

And he pressed the button.

19.

The roar of mighty gears, long at rest, drowned out the blaring alarm. The segmented metal of the fire doors slowly rose up into the rails along the ceiling. Blinding white columns of daylight slid under the fire doors and grew taller as the machinery growled and pulled higher.

The baboon outside the Box was gone. All the baboons in the lab turned to face the opening fire doors, barking, eyes wide, their posture defensive.

Jeff grabbed his gun. It was now or never.

Go!

He threw open the door and sprinted into the lab, running for the exit and the hallway beyond.

"Out, everyone out, now!" He didn't know if anyone was alive to hear him. He wasn't even sure if he spoke the words aloud.

Jeff didn't look back to see if any scientists were evacuating or any baboons were following him. When he reached the lab door, past the mauled bodies of dead guards, he grabbed the handle as he passed and slammed it shut behind him.

His foot hit something, and he went down, rolling onto the hallway's carpeted floor. The fibers were wet, sticky. He rose to his knees, turned around, gun first.

It was Gary. The man's neck was broken, his head lying much too close to his shoulder. Half his chest had been eaten away.

Jeff got up and ran.

"Chris!" he shouted, and this time he was sure he spoke aloud, could feel it tearing itself from his throat and exploding past his lips.

He heard the baboons before he turned the corner. They were still pounding on the day care door, grunting and barking. Jeff could also hear the children's loud whimpers and cries from inside the room.

Leann's body was pushed against the wall opposite the door. Her torso was torn open, her rib cage split down the middle and pulled apart, her organs removed and eaten. A deep red stained the carpet all around her.

Then the baboons saw Jeff.

Jeff stood still.

"You're still hungry?" He clenched his jaw and aimed the handgun at them. "Come and get it."

They ran at him on all fours, their teeth bared. Jeff's foot caught one under the chin, knocking it back. The other leapt at him.

Jeff's body surged with primal strength, the instinct to save his son. He batted the baboon's head with the butt of his pistol, knocking it against the wall. He held the baboon there with one hand, put the pistol to its cheek, and pulled the trigger. A red ichor exploded onto the children's drawings behind its head.

The second baboon rolled onto its feet again and jumped at him. Jeff squeezed the trigger once more. The bullet pierced its throat, passing right through and puncturing the metal fuse box on the opposite wall. The baboon dropped to a heap on the floor as a cascade of fiery sparks erupted from the box.

The lights went out all through the building. The roaring grind of the fire doors stopped. The distant hum of the lab machinery died.

In the windowless hallway leading to day care, Jeff stood in complete darkness.

20.

The children screamed when Jeff kicked in the door. The only light came from the windows in the opposite wall, hitting Jeff right in the eyes. For a moment, the children were just black silhouettes, small hairy heads, and Jeff's brain screamed *baboons!* as he resisted the urge to raise his pistol and fire blindly into the herd.

"Papa!" Chris ran out of the light and into Jeff's arms, sobbing through his eye patch.

Jeff held his boy tight, wanted to hold him like that forever. He felt Chris's back through the thin cloth of his striped shirt, Chris's breath against his neck, the familiar scent of baby shampoo and fabric softener and fresh pure skin that whispered, *This is Chris; this is your son, safe and sound.*

"Papa," Chris said, "Papa, Papa, Papa."

Jeff let go of his son and stood up, addressing the room. "Everyone hold hands," he said. "Single file. Don't let go." Jeff took Chris's hand. "We're getting out of here."

He guided the train of children out the door and back into the pitch-black hallway, straining his eyes against the dark and leading with his gun. "Don't let go," he repeated, his voice low, quiet. He led them around where he remembered Leann's body was, not wanting them to bump into her and create further panic. "Keep your eyes on the person in front of you. Nothing else, okay?"

His shoe touched something heavy. He used his foot to push the limp baboon corpse as far over as he could, then carefully guided the children around it. He could hear the blood-soaked carpet squishing under their feet.

"Don't look anywhere but straight ahead." This time his voice shook a little, and he cursed himself for it.

Jeff could see the corner up ahead where the hallway bent to the right. Dim light emanated from the front door at the far end of that corridor.

"We're almost there," he said, trying to sound confident.

But the doubts were there: what exactly was he leading the children into? Were the baboons still in the building? Would they have been safer locked away in day care until the police arrived?

Jeff forced the thoughts from his head. He knew, on the level of instinct, that he had to get these kids out of there.

"Almost there," he repeated, and they turned the corner into the light.

A lone baboon sat in the center of the hallway, as if it were waiting for them, its small black eyes staring at Jeff from its blue-skinned face. Jeff recognized it right away.

Taylor. The one who taught them to open their cages. The one who attacked Dr. Bradley that morning. The leader.

Their eyes locked.

And something shifted inside Jeff.

He could smell the heady scent of the dusty plains all around him. He felt the dry earth under the soles of his bare feet; the long, polished wood of a spear in his hand. He had no name anymore, no language, just the instinct to survive, to protect the small and weak in his tribe.

"Papa," Chris whined as Jeff let go of his hand.

21.

*W*hat *do the monkey say?*
Monkey say ah-ah.
What do the monkey do?
Monkey go ca-ca.
Who is the monkey man?
Monkey man Papa.

22.

Taylor bared his long teeth, grunted twice, and rose up on all fours.

Jeff also bared his teeth, his pistol leveled before him as he moved warily forward.

Taylor barked and broke into a gallop.

Jeff sprang forward to meet him.

They collided in the air, coming down in a single, twisting heap. Jeff landed on top, but the gun slipped from his hand, bouncing across the carpet and coming to a stop at the far wall.

Taylor's wide hands wrapped around Jeff's throat, his legs wrapping around Jeff's waist. Jeff punched Taylor in the snout, then grabbed the baboon's neck and squeezed.

Fire raging. Drums pounding. Battle for food. Battle for supremacy.

They rolled back and forth along the carpet, each trying to break the other's neck or cut off his air. Jeff grunted, gritting his teeth and straining harder against Taylor's hairy throat.

The trees. The savannah. Man-ape, barely aware of himself as sentient. Nests invaded by marauding troops of baboons, their snouts snapping, hungry for meat. Fight! Protect! Defend!

Taylor's long fingers dug into Jeff's skin, the nails cutting into him. The baboon's teeth inched closer to Jeff's face.

Jeff let go of Taylor's neck and grabbed the baboon's lower jaw with his right hand, his left hand around the upper snout. With all his might, he forced the jaw to open wider, wider. Taylor let go of Jeff's neck and used his hairy fists against the sides of Jeff's head, his strong legs thrashing and kicking. Jeff held on tight, pulling Taylor's jaw farther open, cutting his hands on the baboon's sharp teeth.

A snap, a deep crack, and there was no more resistance. Taylor stopped struggling and weakly pulled himself out from under Jeff's body, his broken jaw hanging loosely open. The baboon tried to pull himself away, tried to find safety, but Jeff pounced on him again.

He put a knee on Taylor's back, grabbed the baboon's head, and twisted, pulling hard. Taylor let out a squeal just before his neck broke. Jeff stayed on top of the baboon's body, prodding it with his hands to make sure it didn't move again.

"Papa?" A tentative voice from behind him.

Jeff whirled around, teeth bare, hands up.

Fight! Protect!

Chris screamed and ran back to the line of frightened, sobbing children. Jeff looked down at his blood-covered hands, at the baboon hair matted to that blood, and came back to himself.

He stood up slowly, breathing hard, trying to compose himself.

"Is everyone all right?" he asked, and his voice, his language, sounded alien to him.

The children all nodded, wide-eyed and terrified.

Jeff picked up his handgun, ejecting the magazine. Three bullets left. He slapped it back in, took Chris's hand, and led them toward the door. He didn't speak. No one did.

23.

Sunlight streamed through the frosted glass of Kiernan Clinical Research's entrance. Jeff glanced back at the line of children behind him, all holding hands and looking at him with such expectation, such hope. He took a deep breath, turned back to the door, and opened it.

The lawn and parking lot outside looked like an earthquake hit. Discarded protest signs lay everywhere. Two police cars straddled the curb; the one in front had collided with a cement garbage receptacle, and the one behind it must have crashed into the first. The doors were open, but there was no sign of the police officers.

Then Jeff saw the dead bodies in the grass, and a few on the asphalt of the parking lot. Some still wore lab coats, but he couldn't tell if any of them were cops. There was too much blood, too much of them eaten away.

The four remaining baboons huddled over the bodies in the grass, their snouts wet and red. They were tearing into Unwashed Mountain Man's corpse, pulling out chunks of meat and stuffing their mouths.

Jeff stood in the doorway, keeping the children behind him.

The baboons caught scent of the children, easy prey, and looked up.

In the distance, Jeff could hear more sirens, but he couldn't tell how far away they were.

What are you going to do now, sport?

Four baboons. Three bullets left.

Jeff squeezed his son's hand.

Go.

(F)EARLESS

During my college years at Sarah Lawrence, I studied folklore with Albert Sadler, who, as A.W. Sadler, wrote extensively on Eastern folklore and religion. In class we paid special attention to Japanese folklore, reading numerous volumes of Lafcadio Hearn's collected folktales, including his most famous, Kwaidan. While all the stories of vengeful ghosts, mischievous shapeshifters, and greedy kappas lit a fire in my mind, none of them stuck with me as vividly as the story of Mimi-Nashi-Hoichi, or Hoichi the Earless. (I'm hardly alone in that, by the way. It's probably the best-known tale in Kwaidan.) In this story, which is original to this collection, I wanted to pay homage to the folktale of Hoichi, and play with it a bit, too. And if I could poke a little fun at the ubiquitous tropes of the cinematic subgenre affectionately known as J-Horror in the process, why not?

1.

Kiyoshi Matsushima swiveled his desk chair to face the window in the trailer wall behind him. Outside, a gloomy gunmetal sky had settled over the clearing in Itabashi where they'd set up for the day's shoot. Perfect weather for the scene, really. It was important that everything be perfect. There was a lot riding on this.

That he'd been hired to direct *Seven Chords*, a big budget movie from a major studio, was nothing short of a miracle, the second chance he'd waited a long time for. Things were about to change for him, he could feel it. They had to. From rock bottom, there was no place to go but up.

The backs of his ears tingled the way they did when he was sure someone was looking at him, and he swung the chair around again.

She stood just inside the doorway, her long, tangled black hair hanging low over her face, obscuring her features save for one milky white eye that peered out at him through the strands. Her arms hung stiffly at her side, her skin as pale and thin as onion paper, dark veins visible beneath the flesh. She wore a ratty white dress, filthy from the grave.

"Show me the walk," Kiyoshi said.

She lifted her arms toward him, fingers groping, and took one lurching step forward, then another.

"Stiffer," he said. "Remember, you've been dead for years. Your joints aren't used to moving anymore. And don't show any emotion. Keep your anger, your need for vengeance, on the inside. You're not a woman anymore, you are *yurei*, an angry spirit, a force of nature. Relentless. Unstoppable." She bent her arms slightly at the elbows and wrists, splayed her fingers into claws, and staggered in circles. "Better," he said. His smartphone buzzed, vibrating its way across the desk. He glanced at it, wondering if it was Asumi, his ex-wife, calling about his weekend plans with Mai, but the name on the display was Yasushi Sato, his assistant director. He picked it up and answered, "Yes?"

"Mr. Matsushima? I'm sorry to disturb you, but I'm at the gate." Yasushi sounded tense, agitated, and extremely apologetic. "Shun Takeda is here."

Kiyoshi leaned forward in his chair. "Don't let him in!"

"He already got past security," Yasushi said. "They didn't know he was banned from the set. We're looking for him now, but he's already inside."

"Damn it!" Kiyoshi ended the call, dropped the phone in his pocket, and stood up. Alarmed by his outburst, the actress staggering around the room parted the long hair in front of her face and peered at him through her white contact lenses. Kiyoshi snatched up his clipboard, snapped, "Come on," and led her out of the trailer.

Outside, the autumn air was brisk. He could smell rain on the wind, an approaching storm, and wondered if they could use it for the scene. It could work. Around the set, the crew was up in the trees on ladders and cranes, clearing the remaining leaves from the branches to give the scenery a more sparse, haunted look. Kiyoshi glanced at his watch, then rubbed his forehead. The last thing he needed was Shun Takeda barging in and slowing everything down. He didn't have time for distractions, not on such a tight schedule.

A knot of tension throbbed behind his eyes. He took a deep breath, remembering the coping techniques Dr. Mizuno had taught him. *When you feel it happening, just close your eyes and breathe deeply. Breathe in the good, breathe out the bad.*

When he opened his eyes, the actress in ghost makeup was looking at him expectantly, waiting to be dismissed. He scanned the papers on his clipboard. "We're shooting scenes forty and forty-one, where you come out of the Shakujii River and confront Toshio on the wooden bridge. I'll need you ready in twenty minutes. Tell makeup the veins need to be darker so they show up on film." She ran off toward a cluster of trailers in the distance, the long black hair of her wig billowing at her shoulders.

A man appeared around the corner of Kiyoshi's trailer, dressed in black jeans and a brown turtleneck sweater. His hair was cut short, and he wore thick, black-rimmed glasses. The man froze as he watched the actress run past, then turned angrily to Kiyoshi. "Please tell me *that's* not in the movie!"

Shun Takeda. Kiyoshi made a mental note to fire the security guards.

"*That,*" he replied, not bothering to hide the contempt in his voice, "is what the audience wants to see. *That* is what got this movie made, not to mention the American distribution and remake deal. *That* is what got you your money, Mr. Takeda."

"It's a joke, that's what it is," Shun said. "Long-haired ghost women? You can't be serious. It's been done to death. It doesn't even belong in the story. That's not what my book is about!"

"We've been over this before," Kiyoshi said. He looked around for security. Why weren't they dragging this annoyance away already?

"My *book* is what got the movie made, not this…," Shun waved his hand toward the actress as she stepped into the makeup trailer, "this *nonsense*. The book was a number one bestseller for a reason, Mr. Matsushima, and that reason is that it was new, it was fresh. It wasn't just the same old ghost women coming out of the water. What's next, scary images on a videotape?"

"Don't be absurd," Kiyoshi said.

Shun reached into his coat. Kiyoshi tensed, wondering if the writer was so far gone that he intended to shoot him, but instead Shun pulled out a copy of his book and offered it to Kiyoshi. "Here, take this. Just promise you'll read it. That's all I ask."

"That's what the screenwriter is for," Kiyoshi said. "If you don't like the adaptation, take it up with him. Or with the studio, for that matter."

"I've already tried. No one will return my calls."

Kiyoshi wasn't surprised. He himself had stopped taking Shun's calls weeks ago. "We're on a tight schedule, Mr. Takeda. We've already got a firm release date, we can't go changing everything now."

Shun forced the book into his hands. "Please. You'll see it's better than the script that studio hack wrote. I know you will. You're the director, you have clout. You can talk to the producers, ask them for a rewrite, get them to push the release date back if you need to."

Kiyoshi almost laughed. Like most authors, Shun had no idea how the film industry worked. There was a reason authors were paid so much for the options on their books. It was supposed to shut them up. Furthermore, there was no way he was going to risk rocking the boat just because Shun was unhappy. He needed this job. He needed everything to go smoothly.

Over Shun's shoulder he saw two large men in black shirts jogging toward him, coiled wires dangling from their ears, and he breathed a sigh of relief. Yasushi Sato ran behind them, struggling to keep up, his young face grimacing nervously. When the security guards slowed to a halt behind Shun, Kiyoshi said, "You know you're not supposed to be here. These men will escort you out."

The guards each put a hand on Shun's shoulders.

"I've devoted my life to this story," Shun said, struggling as they tried to pull him away. "You're destroying it!"

"Get this man out of here," he told Yasushi, who nodded breathlessly. Then Kiyoshi added, to Shun, "If you come to my set again, I'll have you arrested."

He turned and started walking toward the camera crew setting up by the bank of the Shakujii River. Listening to Shun's fading threats and cries of indignation as the guards led him away, Kiyoshi glanced at the book in his hand, a manga with a brightly illustrated cover. On it, a spiky-haired boy was wearing earphones and holding an electric guitar as ghostly shapes congregated behind him. Frankly, it looked awful, which made the words INTERNATIONAL BESTSELLER printed across the bottom all the harder to believe. At the top, the title was written in choppy, bleeding *kanji*: EARLESS. Awful title, he thought. The studio had been smart to change it.

He tucked the book under his arm and shook his head. Every film had its curse. Sometimes it was an impossible actor. Sometimes it was an incompetent crew. With *Seven Chords*, it was Shun Takeda.

2.

Kiyoshi moved his finger along the Tokyo Metro map on the station wall, tracing the blue stripe of the Mita Line from Itabashi Station all the way to where he lived in Shinagawa Ward. He'd had a car once, but it, like so much of his life before the hospital, was gone now, sold to make ends meet during the dry years after his release when he couldn't find work. His last movie, a yakuza thriller, had to be completed by someone else while he was under Dr. Mizuno's care, but even after he was discharged, even after he assured the producers and studio heads there would be no more breakdowns, his phone didn't ring and his savings drained away. No one wanted to hire a director who'd been in a mental institution. Tracing the line on the map was a ritual he performed twice a day, though he knew the route by heart. It reminded him of all he'd lost, and all he hoped to regain.

As the overcast sky darkened into night, he climbed the stairs to the open-air platform and thought of Mai, his daughter, already twelve years old. He'd missed her tenth birthday while in the hospital, something he still couldn't forgive himself for. It had come shortly after Asumi filed the divorce papers. She refused to bring Mai to the hospital, so he'd been forced to send his birthday wishes over the phone. *Happy double digits, Mai. Daddy loves you. I can't wait to see you again,* he'd said into Asumi's voicemail, praying she would deliver the message. In his darkest hours, it had always been the thought of Mai that kept him from slipping irretrievably into despair, and now, knowing he would have her this weekend, he could feel the stress that had been throbbing behind his eyes start to loosen.

He squeezed between the commuters on the crowded platform, making his way to the edge. He peered down the tracks, but there was no sign of the train yet. He sighed, uncomfortable. The platform was filled to capacity, a sea of black hair all around him, interrupted only by the occasional headband or hat. The press of their bodies felt like walls closing in on him. It made him think of other walls, bare white walls in a stark eight-by-twelve room, and a window of tempered glass in the door so the doctors could see in...

He forced the thought from his mind. Room 49 was behind him now, a ghost of the past. The wind of an approaching train drew his attention down the length of track again. As the train rounded the bend, its bright headlights dazzled Kiyoshi's eyes. He looked away, blinking, and at the same moment a sudden commotion arose at the far end of the platform. He glanced over, his vision still spotted with floating white dots, and as the train pulled into the station, he thought he saw a single black pant leg extend out from the platform edge. Then, a flash of brown like polished wood, a shape falling onto the tracks. The screams of the people on the platform were indistinguishable from the piercing shriek of the train's emergency brakes. Commuters shoved past him, surging toward the spot where the shape had fallen. He saw people turn away, hiding their faces, and heard the murmur of the crowd as news of a suicide filtered from one end of the platform to the other.

Stunned, Kiyoshi pulled himself together, and took out his phone to let Asumi know he'd be late. But the screen stayed a vacant, indifferent black. The battery was dead. He pocketed the phone again and looked for a payphone, but couldn't find one. There was no way to reach Asumi. He was supposed to meet her and Mai at his apartment. They would leave when he didn't show up. He wouldn't get his weekend with his daughter.

Kiyoshi closed his eyes against the whirlwind building inside him.

Breathe in the good, breathe out the bad. Anxiety is only fear turned inward.

Be fearless.

3.

The entire Mita Line was shut down after the suicide. Kiyoshi's train was replaced with a shuttle bus that crawled through heavy traffic toward Shinagawa. It dropped him off twenty minutes late to meet Mai and Asumi, just as the storm clouds finally opened. He hurried uphill along the narrow sidewalks, holding his briefcase over his head against the cold, pelting rain.

When he reached his apartment building, a reed-thin, three-story structure on a narrow street packed tight with identical buildings, he was surprised to find Asumi and Mai still waiting. His ex-wife stood stiff as a board, holding an umbrella in one fist. Mai, dressed in a yellow rain slicker and matching hat, fussed with the backpack slung over her shoulders and then noticed Kiyoshi approaching. She muttered a feeble, "Hi, Dad."

Asumi fixed him with an icy glare. "You're late. We had to wait in the rain. Mai can't afford to get sick now, not with exams coming up. If she catches a cold..." She trailed off. She didn't need to finish the threat. She was good at not having to finish threats.

"Sorry," Kiyoshi muttered, though what he wanted to say, what he'd always wanted to say, was, *What kind of woman leaves her husband just when he needs his family the most?* But he already knew the answer: one who was ashamed to be married to a man who went crazy.

"Where were you?" Asumi pressed. No answer would be good enough, he knew, but this was how their conversations went now. Insinuations. Lobbed cannonballs of guilt.

"There was a problem with the train," he said, not wanting to frighten Mai with details of the suicide.

With her free hand, Asumi fussed with the collar of Mai's slicker, even though there was nothing wrong with it. "You should have called," Asumi said. "We've been standing here for nearly half an hour. There was plenty of time to call."

"My phone battery died." Saying it out loud, it sounded like a lie.

Asumi straightened. "You know I didn't have to do this, right? My lawyer said I didn't have to, because of what happened, but I said no, I want Mai's father to be in her life. The least you can do is try not to keep your daughter waiting in the rain."

Because of what happened. She meant the hospital. Her lawyer had said she could declare Kiyoshi unfit for visitation because of his breakdown. Not agreeing to it was the last bit of kindness she'd shown him, a scrap of generosity he knew she would hold over his head forever.

"Go greet your father." Asumi gently nudged Mai forward. The girl shuffled over and hugged him lightly, as if she didn't want to touch him. Asumi said, "I'll be back for her Sunday night. Don't let her stay up too late. She has to study for a math exam." She kissed Mai goodbye, then turned and walked to her car.

Kiyoshi put his arm around his daughter, ushered her inside and up the stairs to his apartment on the top floor. It was much smaller than the expensive three-bedroom they'd lived in as a family. That one had been on a floor so high sometimes they could look out the enormous living room windows and see the lamps of the houseboats moored in distant Tokyo Bay twinkling like stars at night. Kiyoshi changed out of his wet clothes and fixed Mai a dinner of fish and noodles.

"You used to take me to restaurants," she muttered, sulking.

"Is something wrong with your father's cooking?" She didn't answer, and they ate in silence until Mai asked about the movie.

"Did you say it was a monster movie?"

"A ghost story," he said.

"Is the ghost a girl with long hair?" Mai asked around a mouthful of fish.

He smiled. "Of course."

Mai rolled her eyes. She yanked her ponytail free of its elastic and pulled her hair down over her face. She stood up, put out her arms, and pranced stiffly around the table. "I'm going to come out of your teeveeeee," she moaned.

"Sit down and finish your dinner."

Mai tucked her hair behind her ears and sat. "It's so stupid and old."

"It's going to let me take you to restaurants again."

"Why do you like making movies so much anyway?"

He looked up from his plate. "I thought you liked moves."

"But last time..." She trailed off and stole a quick glance at him before staring at her food. He sighed. She knew it was his career that had triggered his breakdown and broken the family apart, she just didn't know how to talk to him about it. She was scared of him, he understood then, and the thought broke his heart.

In his mind, he saw a hallway, institutional cinderblock walls pale green in the light of flickering fluorescent bulbs. At the end of the hall, a door, the number 49 on a brass plate beneath the tempered glass window. This was the kingdom of the mad and the broken, and its king was Dr. Mizuno, who had been so afraid of germs he wore a blue surgical mask around the patients at all times.

"Movies are like moments frozen in time," he told Mai. "You can see things that aren't around anymore, like old buildings and cars. And people, you can see people who aren't around anymore, either."

She nodded but still didn't look at him.

"Everything stays the same. If you watch a movie from fifty years ago, everyone still looks young, even if they're old today. That's the real magic of movies, and that's why I like making them. Nothing changes or comes undone. There's always a happy ending."

"There isn't *always* a happy ending, Dad," she pointed out.

"Well, the best stories have a happy ending."

She finally met his eyes. "Does yours?"

For some reason the question was like a heavy stone on his chest, crushing him, and suddenly he felt out of breath. His heart raced. He closed his eyes, calmed himself, and told her to finish her dinner.

Afterward, in the living room, Mai saw him pull the copy of *Earless* from his briefcase and place it on a shelf. She sprang off the couch and snatched it up. "Oh, cool! Are you reading this, Dad?"

"Someone gave it to me today."

"It's my favorite book! All my friends love it, too!"

Kiyoshi grinned. "Oh yeah? Then you're going to love what I'm about to tell you."

But Mai wasn't listening, she was too excited, and he had to admit, it felt good to see her like this. It had been a long time since she'd been anything but sullen. "Oh my God, Dad, you have to read it! It's about this boy who's really good at playing the electric guitar. His name is…um…" She bit her lip.

"Toshio," he said.

Mai flipped through the pages. "No, it's a weird name." She stopped and said, "Ah! His name is Hoichi!"

Kiyoshi frowned. Hoichi? A memory flitted at the edge of his mind. He'd heard the name before. Then it came to him: *Mimi-Nashi-Hoichi*, Hoichi the Earless. In grade school he'd read the story of the blind biwa player whose ballad of the tragic battle of Dan-no-ura attracted the attention of the spirits of dead Emperor Antoku Tenno and his soldiers. But it was the end of the story that had stuck with him. The memory of a ghost tearing off Hoichi's ears had kept him awake at night until his mother, fed up with his constant anxiety, finally convinced him it wasn't true.

"So Hoichi's awesome with the guitar, like *really* good," Mai continued. She jutted out one hip, mimed holding a guitar, and pinwheeled her arm as though strumming the strings. "BAOWW! He writes this song about some old battle that happened in ancient history, and then these ghosts start showing up. Not stupid long-haired ghost girls, these are different. They're like samurai, and an Emperor all dressed in robes. It turns out they're the ghosts from the battle he was singing about! Then a Buddhist priest tells him the ghosts are going to kill him, and he paints Hoichi all over his body with, like, these magical words that make him invisible to the ghosts. Except the priest forgets to paint his ears, right? So that's all the ghosts see when they come to get him, and they *rip his ears off* before they leave!" She put her hands over her ears and squealed. "It's so gross!"

Shun Takeda had rewritten the story of *Mimi-Nashi-Hoichi* for a modern audience, Kiyoshi realized, but it had all been changed for *Seven Chords*. The Emperor and his soldiers had been replaced with a lone, vengeful female ghost summoned not by the ballad of Dan-no-ura but by mysterious musical notes discovered on a discarded page of sheet music. Even Hoichi's name had been replaced with one the studio thought would be more relatable for a young audience.

"This is what you should make a movie of," Mai said, shaking the manga at him.

Kiyoshi felt lightheaded. "I am. That's the book I'm filming."

"Oh my God!" Mai shrieked, but then her face clouded with confusion, and she flipped through the manga again. "But there's no ghost girl in here. Are you sure this is the right book?"

4.

That night he dreamt of the suicide and woke in the dark, unsure if he'd been stirred from his sleep by the shriek of the train's brakes or a crash of thunder from outside. Rain washed in heavy sheets down his bedroom window, blurring his view of the buildings across the street even as a flash of lightning lit them like a Klieg light. Unable to fall asleep again, he swung his legs out from under the covers. He glanced at the clock on his bedside table. Just past midnight. Damn. His whole night's sleep was shot. A cup of warm tea would put him at ease, he thought. He walked out of the bedroom and into the hallway, and then froze in mid-step.

A shape stood in the kitchen doorway at the far end of the hall, motionless as a statue. He squinted, trying to see in the dark. It was a girl. Her pale arms hung by her side. Her face was shrouded by a mess of long, tangled hair.

"Mai? What are you doing up?"

The girl didn't move.

A small groan came through the living room doorway beside him. He turned and saw Mai sleeping above the covers on the pullout couch, a tangle of black leggings and an Orange Range concert t-shirt.

Kiyoshi turned to the kitchen again, his heart kicking in his chest, but the doorway was empty. He was seeing things, he told himself. He was half sleep, and his mind was still dreaming.

The phone rang, startling him. Kiyoshi ran back into the bedroom and picked up the cordless by his bed before the second ring, hoping it hadn't disturbed Mai.

It was Yasushi Sato. "I'm sorry to be calling so late, but I don't know if you heard."

"Heard what?"

"So you didn't." Yasushi exhaled loudly. "Shun Takeda's dead."

Kiyoshi sat on the edge of his bed. "What happened?"

"He killed himself. Jumped in front of a train at Itabashi Station. From what I gather, it was quite a few hours after we removed him from the set. I don't know what he was still doing there, but he never went home."

Kiyoshi ran his hand through his hair. He remembered the blur of black and brown leaping off the platform, then thought of Shun's black jeans and brown sweater. He shivered. Without knowing it, he'd witnessed Shun's suicide. "God."

"The funeral's set for Monday afternoon," Yasushi continued. "It would be good if you went. If we all did."

Kiyoshi took a deep breath. "We're shooting Monday. The scene in Toshio's house." He glanced at the empty kitchen doorway, and a sudden sense of *déjà vu* came over him.

"I know there was no love lost between you and Shun, but at the very least it would be good PR to shut down the set early and go to the funeral. He was a popular author, after all. Besides, we can still get a lot done Monday morning. I can make the call time earlier."

Kiyoshi stared at the kitchen doorway, trying to figure out what was nagging at him. Something in the script…

"Mr. Matsushima, are you there?"

"Yes," he muttered. "I'll think about it." He ended the call, opened his briefcase on the small desk opposite his bed, and pulled out a copy of the *Seven Chords* script. He flipped through it until he found the scene they were scheduled to film tomorrow. He sat on the bed, staring at the words.

67. INT. TOSHIO'S HOUSE - NIGHT

A long shot down CORRIDOR, facing KITCHEN DOORWAY. Camera PUSHES IN toward KITCHEN as TOSHIO walks past in foreground holding his GUITAR. Camera continues to PUSH IN, and now we see FEMALE GHOST standing in KITCHEN DOORWAY, silent, unmoving, watching him.

Kiyoshi put the script aside and looked at the empty doorway. He rubbed his face, and in the dark behind his eyes he saw the pale green hallway again, could almost hear the buzzing of the fluorescent lights.

He couldn't let it happen again. Not now, not after coming so far.

The next day, Saturday, was a disaster. Kiyoshi was edgy and irritable, snapping at Mai over every little thing. By that night, she was demanding to go home. "This is your home," he told her, but she said she hated him and locked herself in the bathroom, because it was the only room in the apartment with a door. When he called Asumi, the smug disdain in her voice when she agreed to pick up Mai a day early sent a jolt of tension along his spine. Sunday morning, Kiyoshi watched from his apartment window as Mai ran out onto the sidewalk where Asumi was waiting. The girl hugged her mother tight and let herself be escorted to the car. Asumi glanced his way and shook her head with stinging disappointment. Mai didn't turn to look at him once.

He thought his shoulders would buckle from the weight of his failures.

5.

Less than half the cast and crew went with Kiyoshi to the vast cemetery outside of Yokohama, where Shun Takeda was to be buried alongside his parents, and yet standing at the grave even their small numbers made up the majority of mourners. Kiyoshi wasn't surprised. Shun was such an arrogant pain in the ass it was easy to imagine him driving away countless friends and family members in his lifetime.

It made him think of Mai. He'd tried to call her that morning before school. Asumi had answered. *I think it would be for the best if you two took a break for a while,* she'd said, though he knew what she meant was, *There's still something wrong with you. They let you out too soon.*

As the priest chanted, Kiyoshi pulled his coat tighter against the chill. A photograph of Shun, unsmiling and severe behind his black-rimmed glasses, hung on the face of the gravestone. Kiyoshi couldn't take his eyes off it. He'd watched Shun die. It had happened right in front of him.

Why was Shun still in Itabashi at that hour? Why had he stayed?

After the service, Kiyoshi remained by the graveside while Yasushi went ahead to get the rented limousine. A bearded man in a crisp, charcoal gray suit separated from a group of mourners and approached him. "It was good of you to come, Mr. Matsushima," the man said, bowing. "Kenjiro Nagahama. I'm the artist Shun worked with on *Earless.*"

"Good to meet you," Kiyoshi said. He turned back to the gravestone.

Kenjiro sighed. "Shun was always a deeply troubled man. Obsessive. Demanding."

"Tell me about it."

To his surprise, Kenjiro laughed. "It's no secret Shun loathed you. That you came to pay your respects goes a long way."

"Whatever issues he had with me, he's at peace now," Kiyoshi said.

"That would be a first," Kenjiro said. "But no, he took his own life in anger and despair. I have a hard time believing his spirit is resting well."

"You don't really believe in ghosts, do you?"

"I believe in a lot of things, Mr. Matsushima. Don't we all, at funerals? We wish the deceased a peaceful rest. We pay our final respects. On a day like today we all believe in spirits."

Kiyoshi studied the photograph on the gravestone. Shun stared back at him. "He must have been difficult to work with."

"You have no idea," Kenjiro said. "Shun was a perfectionist. If he wasn't in complete control, it infuriated him. He stood over every panel I drew and pointed out everything he thought I was doing wrong. Any mistake, any deviation from his vision, and he would explode and insist I was destroying his story. There were some panels I had to draw nearly a hundred times before he was satisfied. To Shun, the legend of Hoichi was everything. Did you know Shun had a degree in folklore?" Kiyoshi shook his head. "He was obsessed with *Mimi-Nashi-Hoichi*. He devoted his life to studying and interpreting the legend. It became his world. He was convinced the old legends of Japan were being forgotten by each new generation, in danger of being lost forever and replaced with what he called the empty totems of pop culture. It was his idea to reinterpret the story of Hoichi as a manga that would appeal to the younger generation. And it paid off. *Earless* was extremely successful. It made both our careers, and he actually seemed happy for a time, until the movie deal happened."

"Why didn't that make him happy, too?"

"Control issues, remember? The publisher owned the movie rights, but if he'd had his way, there probably never would have been a movie. Especially not yours. He hated what you were doing to the story."

"It would have made him a rich man," Kiyoshi said.

"He was already rich. What he valued was artistic integrity. What he wanted was respect." Kenjiro bowed again. "Good luck with the movie, Mr. Matsushima. I hope it does well for you."

Kiyoshi watched him walk away, then made his own way down the narrow paved path that cut through the cemetery. In the distance, Yasushi waited by the limousine. Kiyoshi walked toward him as the cold wind picked up, biting through his coat and blowing leaves across the ground.

The backs of his ears tingled. He turned, certain someone was watching him, and noticed a woman standing atop a low hill in the distance, shadowed by a leafless tree. The wind rustled the long, tangled black hair in front of her hidden face. Her white dress was torn and dirty, her pale hands bent into claws. At first he thought it was the actress playing the ghost in *Seven Chords*, that for some reason she'd come to the funeral still in her wardrobe and makeup, but then he remembered that she'd taken the day to visit her parents in Nagoya. She hadn't come with them at all. Kiyoshi's mouth went dry.

The woman didn't move. A shape crested the hill behind her and stood at her side. It was another pale woman in a filthy dress, identical to the first. Together they stared at him from behind their hair.

Kiyoshi hurried to the waiting limousine. He dove into the backseat and pulled the door shut. He risked a glance through the tinted window, jabbed his thumb in his mouth and bit down hard, but they wouldn't go away; they kept watching him from beneath the tree. He heard blood rushing in his ears. Heard the slam of the door of Room 49.

Yasushi got in beside him and caught the look in his eye. "Are you okay?"

"Fine, fine. Let's just go."

6.

Kiyoshi was on edge all the next day on set. The sight of the actress in her dirty dress and ghost makeup put a ball of ice in his stomach. He snapped at everyone, actors and crew alike, and by the end of the day they were averting their eyes and talking in hushed tones. He felt like a bomb waiting to explode.

He bought a newspaper to read on the train ride home, hoping it would help him relax. Finding a seat on the crowded train, he leafed through the paper, skimming listlessly through political reports and sports scores until he came across Shun

Takeda's obituary. Each word he read shortened the bomb's fuse. Shun had attended Hokkaido University as a folklore scholar. He never wrote another manga after *Earless*. Rarely did public events or signings. Didn't marry, had no children. Lived alone in Shimonoseki.

One line in particular jumped out at him: *The reclusive author created the internationally bestselling manga with illustrator Kenjiro Nagahama, a Buddhist priest turned artist.*

Kenjiro was a priest? He hadn't mentioned it at the funeral.

Kiyoshi glanced at the passengers packed in around him, holding onto the handles above their heads and swaying with the movement of the train. A cluster of commuters was gathered around a pole in front of him, jostling for space, and through the hive of shoulders and scarves he saw a long cascade of black hair. He stiffened, the newspaper crumpling in his hands. Then he saw it was only a woman with her head bent over a book, and he let out his breath.

Home, he ate a quick dinner and settled in front of the television to watch the dailies he'd burnt to DVD. He wasn't expecting to see anything good, the whole day had been a waste, but he figured focusing his mind on something would help calm him. He slipped the disc into the player and turned on the set.

The screen filled with static. He hit the fast forward button on the remote, and still saw only static. "You're kidding me," he said, annoyed. The static cleared away suddenly to reveal black-and-white footage of a man, his back to the camera, standing at the bottom of the steps to Itabashi Station. Kiyoshi leaned forward on the couch. "What the hell?" He hadn't shot any of this footage.

The man turned around and glanced into the distance, as if he were looking for something. Kiyoshi squinted at the screen in confusion.

It was Shun Takeda.

Shun climbed the steps to the platform, walked to one end, checked his watch. A train came and left, and still Shun remained, waiting for something. Kiyoshi hit the fast-forward button. More trains arrived, departed; crowds swelled on the platform and then drained into the doors; the sky grew progressively darker; and all the while Shun waited. Then, Shun's expression turned angry as something in the crowd caught his attention. Kiyoshi scanned the commuter's faces, trying to find what Shun had seen, and he caught a glimpse of—

Himself.

He was the one Shun had been waiting for. That was why Shun had stayed in Itabashi. He'd *wanted* Kiyoshi to witness his suicide.

The image on his TV flickered, jumped, and Itabashi Station disappeared. In its place was a cinderblock corridor, lit from above by flickering fluorescent tubes, and at the end of the hall, a door marked 49.

Then static again. Kiyoshi watched it drift across the screen like snow. He tried to remember the coping techniques Dr. Mizuno had taught him, but suddenly he couldn't. After a minute, he managed to get off the couch and turn off the TV. He removed the DVD carefully, afraid to touch it. Written in black marker across the top, in his own handwriting, were today's date and the scene numbers they'd shot. Impossible. Where had the images come from? How had they gotten on the disc?

It plagued him well into the night, keeping him from sleep. When he did finally drift off, a loud crash in the bedroom woke him immediately. Terrified, he glanced around the room and thought he saw a ragged shape moving through the darkness, but when he worked up the courage to switch on the bedside lamp his room was empty.

He sprang out of bed and searched the room, but there was nothing. He felt like a fool. He had to pull himself together. There was too much at stake to let himself come undone now.

Through the window, movement caught his eye. Two women stood in the street below. Long, tangled black hair hid their faces, but he knew they were looking at him. Another woman, identical to the others, walked stiffly out of the shadows to join them, and then there were three staring up at his window.

7.

The phone was ringing. It had been ringing all day. Kiyoshi sat at the dining table with his knees drawn up to his chest. He couldn't answer the phone because the phone was in the bedroom, and so was she. She'd been standing by his bed when he woke in the morning, wild black hair hanging over her face.

This wasn't another breakdown. He knew that now. This was all Shun's fault. It had started with Shun's death, the suicide he'd forced Kiyoshi to witness. The writer's angry spirit was haunting him.

The phone stopped ringing. How many calls did that make now? Five? Six? He could guess who it was: Yasushi Sato, wondering why he wasn't on set. Had Yasushi called the studio yet? Was there already an angry message threatening to take him off the movie? *We shouldn't have hired you, Mr. Matsushima. They let you out too soon.* He couldn't let them do that. *Seven Chords* was all he had left.

Kiyoshi rose from the chair and peered down the hall toward his bedroom doorway. The room beyond looked quiet. He crept closer, desperate not to make a sound. If she heard him, she would come to the door and stare at him from behind her hair, and he couldn't handle that, he just couldn't. He peeked slowly inside the room, and found it empty.

He sat on the bed, picked up the cordless, and dialed his voicemail. A half dozen messages from Yasushi clogged his mailbox, ranging from annoyed to concerned. Kiyoshi figured he should call him, tell him to send everyone home. He could make up an excuse why he wasn't there, a cold, a migraine, anything but the truth. No one would believe him. He'd be sent back to Room 49, but this time they'd be wrong. This time it wasn't his fault.

He was about to dial Yasushi's number when the phone rang in his hand. The display showed Asumi's name. Why was his ex-wife calling him? He hit the talk button. "Asumi?"

Only static answered him.

"Mai?" Kiyoshi sat up straight. More static. "Mai, is that you?"

He thought someone spoke then, but he couldn't hear what they said. Long strands of black hair had begun to push out of the tiny speaker holes at the top of the phone. The hair kept flowing out, dangling lower, lower. It touched his hand, dry and brittle like straw, and brushed against the sensitive skin of his wrist.

Kiyoshi screamed and dropped the phone. He scuttled backward and fell off the bed, knocking a pile of papers off his desk. Something heavy dropped onto his hand. The copy of *Earless* Shun had given him. Hadn't he put it on the shelf in the living room? How had it gotten into his bedroom? The book had fallen open, he saw, its two halves straddling his fingers like a tent. He picked up the manga, his thumb slipping between the open pages, and turned it over.

The page where it had fallen open showed only a single panel of a hand holding a telephone. Thick, gooey ectoplasm oozed out of the handset and down the character's arm. Kiyoshi glanced at the phone he'd dropped. The hair was gone. Then he looked again at the almost identical scene on the page.

Kiyoshi thought of what Shun said as he'd put the manga in his hands: *Just promise you'll read it. That's all I ask.* Was that what this was about? Was that all Shun's spirit wanted of him, to read the book?

Taking it into the living room, he sat with his legs crossed on the couch, a cup of hot tea on the coffee table to soothe his nerves, and read *Earless* front to back, taking in Shun's words and Kenjiro's artwork. The story was just as Mai had described it, and filled with details Kiyoshi remembered from when he'd read the legend of Hoichi as a boy. He stopped when he turned a page and saw a ghostly samurai standing in a doorway at the end of a long corridor, just like the first ghost woman Kiyoshi had seen. His pulse quickened. He read on, and soon came across a panel where two spirits dressed as samurai watched Hoichi from a cemetery hilltop, beneath the shadow of a leafless tree. His hands trembling, he kept reading, and stopped again when he saw Hoichi looking out the window of his apartment at night. Three spirits, the one in center dressed in the regalia of an Emperor, stood on the street below, staring up at him.

Kiyoshi turned the page and nearly dropped the book. There, in crisp black ink, was Hoichi, sitting cross-legged on his couch and reading a book exactly as Kiyoshi was, a cup of tea in exactly the same place on the coffee table. A box of text in the corner of the panel revealed what the boy was reading: *Hoichi, with the holy sutra painted across his body to keep him invisible to the spirits, heard the ghostly samurai's rage at not being able to find him. Suddenly he felt his ears gripped by fingers as cold and hard as iron, and torn from his head. Great as the pain was, he gave no cry to alert the spirit to his presence. As the heavy footfalls receded and vanished, Hoichi felt warm, thick blood trickling from where his ears had been. The only places on his body where the priest had forgotten to paint the sutra.*

The end of the manga was the same as the legend, Hoichi losing his ears to the ghosts. That, too, had been changed for the movie. In the *Seven Chords* script, Toshio sacrificed himself to stop the vengeful ghost from killing his friends, electrocuting himself with a faulty guitar amp. Kiyoshi closed the book and looked again at the cover illustration of the teenage guitarist. Only now did he notice the slight trickle of blood coming out from under the boy's earphones.

Was that enough? Would the haunting end now because he'd read Shun's manga? Or did Shun want him to admit the book was better than the script?

"It is," he said to the empty room. "You were right. It's better."

The room stayed silent. Nothing moved. No hair grew out of his tea, no ghost women emerged from the cracks in the walls. Maybe it was over. Maybe that was all Shun had needed to rest in peace.

But that night, as Kiyoshi slept, it became clear nothing was over. He dreamt of the suicide again, only this time it was he himself who leapt in front of the oncoming train. A platform full of ghostly women watched him, crowded together like a sea of long black hair. When he woke, his heart was pounding in his chest like he'd just run a marathon, and he understood.

Shun Takeda wanted him dead.

Frustrated, Kiyoshi flipped through *Earless* again. If the manga was so important to Shun, the answer had to be in there somewhere. He'd simply missed it the first time through. He turned page after page and paused when he reached Hoichi's meeting with the Buddhist priest. Kiyoshi looked closer and realized Kenjiro had drawn his own face on the priest. An inside joke, he figured, a reference to the fact that the illustrator had once been a Buddhist priest himself.

And suddenly Kiyoshi knew what he had to do. He jumped off the couch and ran for the phone.

8.

Kenjiro opened the door of his small house, frowned at Kiyoshi, and said, "You look terrible."

"He won't let me sleep," Kiyoshi said. "He won't give me a moment's peace." He followed Kenjiro into the living room. All the furniture had been pushed to the walls, he noticed, and a large bamboo mat and six clay bowls had been set up in the middle of the room.

Kenjiro motioned for him to sit on the mat. "I'm not surprised. Bad dreams, hallucinations, spirits have the power to get inside your head and make you see what they want you to see."

Kiyoshi thought of the train ride he'd taken on his way to Kenjiro's house. Ghostly, long-haired women had stood on every platform they passed. "I didn't think you would believe me."

"I told you, I believe a lot of things. When Shun took his own life, he was furious at you, and that fury still burns inside him." He sat across from Kiyoshi on the mat and picked up a tapered horsehair brush from the floor beside the bowls.

"He wants to kill me," Kiyoshi said.

"Anger is all he knows now. But I think I can help you." Kenjiro picked up one of the bowls. A viscous black liquid swirled inside. He dipped the brush into it. "Remove your clothes."

Kiyoshi unbuttoned his shirt. "You're sure this will work?"

Kenjiro smiled. "It worked for Hoichi, didn't it?" He moved the brush to Kiyoshi's chest and painted a small *kanji* there, then another. The ink was cold against Kiyoshi's skin.

"But it's not true, is it?" Kiyoshi asked while Kenjiro continued painting. "The legend of Hoichi, I mean?"

Kenjiro shrugged, squinting at his work. "Who's to say whether a legend is true or not? All that matters is that it's told, and remembered. Shun understood that more than anyone."

Kiyoshi glanced around the floor but didn't see any scrolls or sheets of paper for Kenjiro to work from. "You know the sutra by heart?"

"I was a Buddhist priest for many years. The *Hannya-Shin-Kyo* was drilled into us."

Kiyoshi chuckled. It felt good to laugh again. "I've never heard of a priest becoming a manga artist before."

Kenjiro sighed. "Money can make you do strange things. My family was poor and needed help. As a priest I couldn't earn money to send back home, but with my art I could. So I left the priesthood, and before I knew it a dozen years had passed and I had built a career. I never went back."

"I'm sorry."

"We all make sacrifices," Kenjiro said. "We do what we can to help others. It's why I became a priest in the first place."

Painting the sutra over his body was a painstaking process. Kiyoshi sat, and at times stood, perfectly still, trying to ignore the humiliation of his nakedness. Kenjiro drew letter after letter over him, each one abutting the next so that no patch of skin went uncovered. "And your ears," he said as Kiyoshi felt the pointed tip of the brush dab his earlobe. "We don't want to make the same mistake Hoichi did. There, now we just have to wait for the ink to dry."

"And then?" Kiyoshi asked.

"Then you'll do as Hoichi did. Go home and wait for Shun to come again tonight."

Kiyoshi looked at his painted arms, the thick black *kanji* of the sutra bending and warping over his muscles and bones. He touched his face, felt the sticky ink on his cheeks and forehead. "I can't ride the train home like this."

Kenjiro retrieved a keyring from one of the tables against the wall. "You can borrow my car. When you get home, sit perfectly still, no matter what you see or hear. In order for this to work, you mustn't make eye contact with Shun, and under no circumstances should you speak, even if he demands it."

Kiyoshi looked at his own painted chest. Suddenly, it all seemed absurd. "You're sure he won't be able to see me?"

"Absolutely," Kenjiro said. "If he can't find you, his anger won't have a focus and his spirit will move on. I promise you, by tomorrow morning this will be over."

The sun was setting by the time the ink dried. Kiyoshi thanked Kenjiro and took the artist's car. As he drove, he saw the letters upon his hands on the steering wheel, caught glimpses of them on his face in the rearview mirror, and wondered what he was doing. Was a dead man really haunting him? The hallucinations, the nightmares, he'd experienced them before without the luxury of believing an angry spirit wanted him dead. He pulled to the side of the highway and rested his head against the steering wheel. How had he let this happen? How had he slipped so far into madness without realizing it? No wonder his marriage had crumbled. No wonder his daughter wanted nothing to do with him.

After a few minutes, he gathered himself and pulled the car back into traffic. It was already dark when he arrived. He opened the door and stepped into a hallway of plain cinderblock walls and a hard cement floor. Fluorescent lights hummed along the ceiling, casting a greenish tint on his surroundings. At the far end of the hall, an open door waited for him, and beyond it he saw the bare plaster walls and stark wooden furniture of Room 49.

He took a deep breath and tried to breathe out the bad. There never should have been a Room 49. Not those numbers together. *Shi* and *ku*. Death and agony.

And yet, even after Dr. Mizuno had discharged him, Kiyoshi always knew he'd be back one day.

The cement floor was no longer bare. Now it was covered with a brittle mat of long black hair that crunched and rolled under his feet.

It wasn't real, he told himself. Nothing he'd seen was real. It was only his anxiety, his fear turned inward.

Be fearless.

As he walked toward his room, he peeled off his clothes. He didn't deserve them. They were the clothes of a man, and he was not a man. He was a failure. A failure as a filmmaker. A failure as a husband. A failure as a father. Naked at the end of a trail of discarded clothing, he sat in the middle of Room 49 and listened to the familiar click of the door as it closed behind him. To one side was the narrow, wood-framed bed he remembered. To the other, the scrubbed metal sink and toilet. Before him, the comforting blank whiteness of the wall. This room, more than anywhere else, was where he belonged. Kenjiro had told him to go home, and so he had.

The backs of his ears tingled. Someone was behind him. He hadn't heard the door open. He turned and saw a man standing by the door. Kiyoshi turned away quickly, ashamed. "Hello, Dr. Mizuno."

"I was hoping I wouldn't see you back here," Dr. Mizuno said. His footsteps drew closer. "What have you done to yourself?" A hand touched Kiyoshi's shoulder. The fingers felt cold, spongy. Latex gloves. Dr. Mizuno and his germ phobia. "Are these words? *Hannya-Shin-Kyo*," he read off Kiyoshi's skin. Then he laughed. "The holy sutra? Am I to call you Hoichi now?"

Kiyoshi shuddered at the name, and at the doctor's probing touch.

"You shouldn't have let it get this bad before coming to see me," Dr. Mizuno continued. "I read with some concern about you directing another movie. I warned you to find another line of work, didn't I? Something that wouldn't set you off again?"

Kiyoshi was too ashamed to answer.

"I can't help you if you won't talk to me," Dr. Mizuno said. "Why did you take this film, after everything we discussed? Why, when you knew the risk, would you undo all the work we did together?"

He thought of Asumi calling the hospital to tell him she was leaving him. He thought of Mai saying that she hated him. "To prove that I could," he said.

"Prove to whom?"

"Mai, Asumi, the studios. Everyone."

Dr. Mizuno came around from behind and squatted before him, his white doctor's coat billowing out over his knees. A blue surgical mask covered the lower half of his face. "No, that's not it."

"No one wanted me when I left here," Kiyoshi said. "Not the studios, not my wife, not my own daughter. Everyone thought I was crazy."

"Are you?"

"No," he insisted. "But something's wrong with me. I've been seeing things."

"Was it worth it?" the doctor asked. "Taking this stupid movie that wouldn't even be as good as the book? Was it worth it to be so selfish, so stubborn?"

Kiyoshi glanced up, met Dr. Mizuno's eyes, and saw only cruelty there.

"You didn't do it for anyone but yourself," Dr. Mizuno continued. "You wanted to show everyone, no matter what the cost. You brought this on yourself."

"That's not true," Kiyoshi insisted. "Directing is the only thing I've ever been good at. It's all I know how to do. What choice did I have?" But even as he said it, he knew it wasn't the whole truth. What he'd wanted was for everything to go back to the way it had been before the first breakdown. For everything that had come undone to be mended, all the cuts in his life spliced back together, his career, his family. He thought there could be a happy ending.

"You're pathetic," Dr. Mizuno said. "You're a liar and a coward."

Kiyoshi blinked back tears. "Why are you talking to me like this?"

Dr. Mizuno stood, shaking his head with disgust. "You think you're an artist? You're a hack. What do you understand of artistic integrity? What do you know of the sacrifices an artist makes for his art?"

"You're supposed to be helping me," Kiyoshi said. Dr. Mizuno started walking toward the door, out of Kiyoshi's line of sight.

"There's no salvation here," Dr. Mizuno said. Kiyoshi heard the snap of the doctor pulling off his latex gloves. "Kenjiro warned you not to speak. You should have listened."

Kiyoshi stiffened.

The walls of Room 49 melted away, and he saw his own living room around him. When the man behind him spoke again, it wasn't with Dr. Mizuno's voice.

"No more rewrites, Mr. Matsushima. No more long-haired ghost women. The empty totems of pop culture have no place here. *This* is how the story goes. And this is how it ends. This is how it always ends. Nothing is more important than that."

Hands as cold and hard as iron gripped Kiyoshi's ears, and began to pull.

ABOUT THE AUTHOR

Nicholas Kaufmann is a critically acclaimed author of horror and dark fantasy whose works have been nominated for the Bram Stoker Award, the Shirley Jackson Award, and the Thriller Award. He lives in Brooklyn, NY with his wife and two ridiculous cats. Visit his website at nicholaskaufmann.com.

BIBLIOGRAPHY

Chasing the Dragon
Die and Stay Dead
Dying Is My Business
General Slocum's Gold
Hunt at World's End
In the Shadow of the Axe
Still Life: Nine Stories

Curious about other Crossroad Press books?
Stop by our site:
http://store.crossroadpress.com
We offer quality writing
in digital, audio, and print formats.

Enter the code FIRSTBOOK
to get 20% off your first order from our store!
Stop by today!

www.ingramcontent.com/pod-product-compliance
Lightning Source LLC
Chambersburg PA
CBHW061231170626
46809CB00007B/2622